UNE**X**PLAINED

SPINE-TINGLING TALES
from **REAL PLACES** around Britain and Ireland

retold by
KAREN LIEBREICH

Illustrations by Sally Townsend

MACMILLAN

First published 1997 by Macmillan Children's Books
a division of Macmillan Publishers Limited
25 Eccleston Place, London SW1W 9NF
and Basingstoke

Associated companies throughout the world

ISBN 0 330 34105 7

3 5 7 9 8 6 4 2

A CIP catalogue record for this book is available from
the British Library.

Printed by Mackays of Chatham plc, Kent

ACKNOWLEDGEMENTS

Many thanks to Dorothy Levy, Debbie Ruff and Shane Hartley who all read the stories with critical eyes. Kevin Brownlow took a break from silent film and proved a mine of generous information on obscure locations. Paul Kriwaczek not only raided his capacious library and memory for stories, but even more importantly provided a telephonic lifebelt in a sea of school runs, broken nights and dirty nappies. Needless to say, I have ignored their opinions where they conflicted with my own, so all remaining errors of fact and judgement are unfortunately my own.

The following people good-naturedly allowed themselves to be pestered by me and responded warmly with advice or information, for which many thanks: the Coldstream Tourist Information Office, Shona Eddington (British Tourist Authority), Colin Johnston (Bath), Dr John Todd (St Bees), Helen Nicholson (Sawston Hall), George Harrison and Jane Darnell (Kirkby Lonsdale), Annette Morris (Lake District), Sally Stephens (Combe Sydenham), Diane Inglis (Spindlestone Heugh), Gudrun Leonard (Bisham Abbey), Harry Riley (Woolacombe), Jan Droy (Winchcombe), Liz de Keyser (Royal Botanic Gardens), Sonja Johnston (The Tower of London), David Timpson and David Marriott (Edinburgh) and Lucy Hollier (Weathampstead).

Sam and Hannah can read this (if they wish) when they get older, but no thanks to them that it has been completed. But to Jeremy for feeding me and financing me, and taking time out from the joys of glomerulonephritis and other exotic diseases, many thanks as always.

AUTHOR'S NOTE

At the end of most of the stories there are directions on how to find the location and further historical information. The vocabulary of these explanatory sections may be more advanced.

If you intend to visit the sites of any of the stories, always try to ring first if possible. For some of the more obscure sites, the Tourist Boards of the relevant areas should be able to help.

The stories are based on historical fact or legend, but inevitably some of them are truer than others. As a general rule, the modern characters and the ghosts and monsters can be assumed to be fictional, though not necessarily of the author's creation, while the historical characters are based on real people. The notes at the end of each story give further details.

CONTENTS

ENGLAND

IRELAND

NORTHERN IRELAND

SCOTLAND

WALES

BATH

PRINCE BLADUD AND THE PIGS OF BATH

850 BC

O ne day, when Prince Bladud looked in the mirror as usual to admire himself, he was horrified to see a small mark on his cheek. Surely not a spot! He never had spots. On the contrary, he had clear skin, longish curly hair and dazzling blue eyes, and he was considered, especially by himself, to be the handsomest young man in the kingdom. He decided to ignore the mark, but the next day it had grown and there was another on his chin. The court doctor was summoned and gloomily announced – this was no ordinary outbreak of pimples. This was leprosy!

King Hudibras, Prince Bladud's father, immediately banished the doctor from his kingdom and summoned another. The new doctor, aware of the fate which had befallen his colleague, was more wary. "It does look very like leprosy," he agreed hesitantly. "I can see why my friend made this mistaken diagnosis. But it is only chickenpox." The doctor was handsomely rewarded and smiled nervously.

But soon it became clear that Bladud's disease was not chickenpox. It looked much worse, and it certainly felt much worse. His handsome looks had completely disappeared. No one would talk to him or play with him for fear of catching the terrible infection.

Finally Prince Bladud himself brought the matter up with King Hudibras.

"Father, you know it is leprosy. What shall I do?"

"Nonsense, nonsense," blustered the King, but secretly he had already sent for the first doctor to return.

King Hudibras could hold out no longer. His courtiers refused to stay in the same room with Prince Bladud. The prince's friends had been sent on long "holidays" by their parents to keep them out of danger. Foreign kings cancelled their visits. King Hudibras summoned the Prince.

"My son," he said sadly, "I'm afraid you must leave court. Your disease is awful and infectious. I can no longer endanger my people with your presence. You may say farewell to your mother from the courtyard, but she may not come down and kiss you." And he waved his son away, his own eyes full of tears.

From the top of the stairs in the courtyard, Queen Alaron wept bitterly as she called farewell to her son. A row of terrified soldiers stood at the steps, hoping that Prince Bladud would not attempt to approach his mother. They would certainly have let him through, rather than touch him and risk infection. Through her sobs, the Queen pulled off a beautiful ruby ring and threw it to him. Bladud caught it, thinking what a useless present it was, and left the castle in a sad and bitter mood.

X X X

After some years of wandering, always shunned and alone because of his unpleasant appearance, Bladud had no money left. He had spent all his father had given him and no one would give him a job, partly because as a king's son he could do very little except rule and fight, but mainly because he looked so terrible.

The disease had spread all over his body. He was covered in itchy sores, flaking white and red from head to foot. His hair was unkempt and dirty, his clothes in rags, and he no longer looked or felt anything like the handsome young prince he had once been.

One day he stopped at a farm near Keynsham to ask for some water, for it was hot and he was thirsty. The farmer was happy to let Bladud drink from the well, and he was so short-sighted he did not even notice Bladud's disease (there were no glasses in those days). They started to chat and the farmer mentioned that he was looking for a new swineherd to look after his pigs. He was very proud of his pigs, six huge beauties, pink and glistening, and needed very little encouragement to introduce Bladud to them.

In no time at all, Bladud found himself appointed as the new swineherd. His job was to feed the pigs, and clean out their pens. It was a long way from palace life but it was better than nothing and the pigs were companionable enough. That is, all except one whom the farmer called Cordelia, the naughtiest pig. She would never leave her pen when he needed to clean it, and she would never go back in when he had finished. She would look him in the eye and overturn her food deliberately. But if he scratched her back just above the shoulder blade she would look up at him adoringly. It was a love-hate relationship.

But one day, while scratching her back, he noticed to his horror that she had broken out in spots. She had caught his disease! Within a few weeks all the pigs were covered in the sores, and

Bladud was terrified the farmer would find out. He requested permission to take the pigs to the opposite side of the river, claiming that the grazing for the pigs would be better over there. Thus the pigs would be out of the farmer's sight for as long as possible.

Needless to say, Cordelia would not come, and made a terrible fuss as Bladud tried to herd her out of her pen. When she finally understood that he was offering her liberty and a life spent snuffling amongst the oak trees in the forests, she galloped out squealing with joy.

Her happiness, however, was short-lived. The pigs' disease became worse and worse. They had no time to eat the delicious acorns, they were so busy scratching their scabs along the tree trunks. Even Cordelia, once so fat, now looked like a bag of bones. Together Bladud and his pigs wandered far and wide, ill, thin and miserable as the disease grew worse.

One cold winter's day Cordelia, itching and irritable, found a pool of black, foul-smelling mud and plunged in. Bladud called her and called her, but all that happened was that the other pigs jumped in too. Cursing, he realized he too would have to enter the freezing water and drag her out. Gingerly he picked his way past the prickly brambles, through the reeds, and dipped his foot in the slimy, algae-covered pond. Strangely enough, it was warm to the touch and there was even steam rising from it. But it certainly reeked of rotten eggs.

"Typical Cordelia," he growled, "to choose such a smelly pond to bathe in." Nor did she want to come out. Eventually, after a mammoth struggle, during which Bladud was covered from head to foot in evil-smelling mud, he managed to entice her out by waving a bag of acorns under her nose. The other pigs soon followed.

Muttering furiously Bladud led his herd to a clear stream and began to wash himself and his animals clean. Cordelia stared at him smugly. She felt much better. For the first time in ages her

4

skin did not itch. She could concentrate on those delicious-looking acorns…

Bladud meanwhile was looking at his arms in amazement. Where he had been covered in mud, his skin was healed! The flaking patches had washed off to reveal healthy skin underneath. Bladud ran back to the muddy pool, stripped off his clothes and dived in head first. A tadpole wriggled down his neck and a water-beetle scuttled over his shoulder but he did not care. He cavorted in joy. "I'm well! I'm better! I can go home!"

Donning his clothes once more, he searched for his herd of pigs, but they seemed to have disappeared. Then, unable to contain himself any longer, he set off back to his father's castle, skipping with happiness.

At the castle gates, men-at-arms barred his way. "What does a ragged beggar like you want with the King?" they asked him roughly, and jeered as they pushed him away.

Suddenly Bladud saw his old doctor approaching the gate. He was to visit the Queen who had been unwell since the banishment of her son. "Doctor, doctor," he called and approached the elderly man. "Pray take this medicine to my lady, the Queen. I promise you it will make her better."

The doctor looked suspiciously at the young man. He seemed rather familiar, but the doctor could not quite place him. His clothing was too poor for him to have ever been a patient of the famous doctor. But the doctor was desperate to find a cure for the Queen, or he risked being sent away into exile once more by the impatient King. He looked down at the young man's hand, and gasped when he saw the brilliant ruby ring. It sparkled in the pale winter sunlight as the young man thrust it towards him.

"Please, just show it to her. I'm sure she will reward you," he cried eagerly, and as the doctor took the ring, Bladud settled down to wait, eyed askance by the men-at-arms.

Within a few minutes the Queen, running faster than she had moved in years, flung the soldiers out of the way and rushed to embrace her son. Without a moment's hesitation, she recognized the ragged figure waiting quietly by the wall. The happiness and festivities were great that evening in the palace of King Hudibras.

Bladud sent out a search party for the pigs, and they were eventually located – back at the pool.

Several years later, when Bladud became king, he built a palace near the mud pool. He cleared off some of the slime and algae and made the pool more pleasant to swim in. This was the foundation of the city of Bath, still famous today for its springs and water. The pigs had a special enclosure at the bottom of the garden, with direct access to the baths whenever they felt like having a wallow. And whenever Bladud felt too arrogant and royal, he would go down and have an argument with Cordelia.

If you go to Bath today, you can see the Roman baths, built over the pigs' pool, and you can taste the water in the Pump Room above. Go to a road called the Circus, built two and a half thousand years after Bladud ruled (around 850 BC), and if you look up, the top balustrades are crowned with acorns, in memory of the pigs' favourite meal.

Incidentally, Bladud was the father of King Lear, about whom Shakespeare wrote a famous play, and was one of the earliest men to attempt to fly using a pair of wings, unfortunately unsuccessfully.

BERKSHIRE

A POOR STUDENT: BISHAM ABBEY

16TH CENTURY

"For goodness' sake, William," said Lady Hoby. "Why can't you sit down and do your homework properly, like other children."

William sighed and hung his head. He did try, honestly he did. But he just could not manage it. Try as he might, he could not seem to please his teachers. His mother, Lady Hoby, was a very clever woman, a friend of the brilliant Queen Elizabeth I, and like the Queen she was excellent at languages and mathematics. She wrote poetry in Latin and even in Greek. She was determined her son should do well too, but poor little William could not get anything right.

Every line he wrote had an ink blot from his quill. Every Latin sentence had at least one mistake, every mathematics exercise added up wrong. At first Lady Hoby thought it was the fault of his teachers, and sacked them one after another. She cut down on his sport – no more riding, no more practising with his sword. Just study, study, study. Eventually she decided to teach him herself, and organized a rigid set of lessons. But William still made little progress, and she soon became sure he was doing it on purpose.

The problem was, the more nervous he became the more stupid he seemed to be, and his mother started to beat him when he made a mistake. The head groom who ran the stables where William used to go riding tried to intervene, but was told to mind his own business or he would be sacked.

Gradually, deprived of sport and fresh air, and desperate about his studies, William grew pale and depressed. The beatings grew worse. Lady Hoby simply could not understand that she, a clever woman, had a son who was not interested in studying and could not do it properly even if he tried for all he was worth. Finally one day, absolutely furious, she hit the boy so hard he never woke up again.

Only then did the realization of what she had done finally dawn on Lady Hoby. "What have I done?" she cried. "Oh, William, William, forgive me."

But there was no answer.

X X X

Lady Hoby could not forgive herself. She fell ill, and she too soon died. But still she had no rest from her terrible deed. Ever since her ghost has appeared around the house, trying to wash her hands which are covered in ink blots in a black inky bowl which floats in front of her, just out of reach, as she wanders around. She is dressed in black with a very white face and hands, and many people have seen her in the house and along the river bank.

Hundreds of years later, in 1840, when workmen came to change the shutters in the schoolroom they discovered several sheets of paper and exercise books, all covered in blots and mistakes, which poor little William had stuffed down between the shutter and the wall, to try and hide them from his stern mother.

Bisham Abbey, in Berkshire, is near Marlow, in Buckinghamshire, about four miles from Junction 8/9 of the M4, and now belongs to the Sports Council. A picture of Lady Hoby hangs in the Great Hall, and the frame is said to be empty when she walks.

You can play sport at Bisham Abbey, or view it from the towpath on the other side of the Thames. The Abbey is fully open to the public once a year on Heritage Open Day.

CAMBRIDGESHIRE

MARY TUDOR AND THE HOLE:
SAWSTON HALL

1553

Mrs Huddlestone's maid, Eva, drew aside as the lady in grey walked slowly down the long gallery. She was a common sight and Eva was not at all frightened. She had seen the ghost, Mary Tudor, many times in the sixty years since she had come to the Hall to work. Later that night, as she settled into bed, she heard the ghostly nightwatchman calling "All's well", as he did every night at midnight on the dot. Soon the Hall was to become a college where foreign students could learn English. She wondered what the two ghosts would think of that.

x x x

It was summer 1553. The young King Edward VI, who had always been a sickly boy, died on 6 July. A goldsmith, Robert Raynes, heard the news from a friend of his who worked at the palace and ran home and told his wife.

"I must warn the King's sister, the Lady Mary," he said. "She's the rightful Queen, but that Duke of Northumberland is hoping to put Lady Jane Grey on the throne!"

His wife prepared some food for him while Robert saddled his horse. Within a very short time he was riding as fast as he could for Thetford, where Mary Tudor was staying. If she did not act swiftly the powerful Duke of Northumberland would put the wrong person on the throne – Lady Jane, who just happened to be married to his own son.

The goldsmith galloped all night and reached Thetford exhausted. As soon as his news was confirmed, Mary declared herself the Queen of England. She called her men to her and within days loyal Catholic friends had ridden to join her. She set off for London, and on the way she stayed the night at Sawston Hall which belonged to one such friend, John Huddlestone. Meanwhile, in London, Lady Jane was declared Queen.

Sawston Hall was a very comfortable house, and Mary was made very welcome. John Huddlestone was a kind man and a good Catholic. After he had bid her goodnight, Mary found she still could not sleep. She was too excited and worried about what would happen, and found herself walking up and down the long gallery, planning what to do. Centuries later Eva, the maid, and many others would see her ghost walk this gallery.

England was split between those who supported the new Protestant religion and those who preferred the old Catholic religion. Feelings ran high. While Mary was the lawful heir, many felt her Catholic religion meant she would not make a good Queen.

The next day, the students and townspeople in nearby Cambridge, which was fervently Protestant, discovered that Catholic Mary was staying with the Huddlestones just a few miles away. Within a couple of hours a huge crowd of people was making its way towards Sawston. John Huddlestone rushed into the room where Mary was working with her advisors.

"Your Majesty," he cried. "We must leave immediately. The mob is on its way here. You are no longer safe in this house."

Mary calmly stood up. She nodded to her servants to follow her immediately and joined John. In the stables the grooms were already saddling the horses. Side by side the Queen and John Huddlestone, accompanied by her other servants and advisers, left the house and galloped through the forest to escape. At a safe distance from the house, the party drew up and turned back to look at Sawston Hall. They had emerged from the forest, and stood in a small clearing on a hill. They could still hear faint shouting from the angry crowd, but of the house itself there was no sign. All they could see were the flames of a huge fire, lighting up the sky for miles around.

John Huddlestone watched with a heavy heart. The house had been beautiful and his pride and joy. Mary stood and watched the flames, and then turned to him.

"John Huddlestone," she said, "I promise you that when I am Queen you shall have a new house every bit as beautiful. I shall not forget what you have done for me."

X X X

Queen Mary Tudor kept her word. On 3 August, not even a month after her brother's death, she entered London in triumph. A few days later the Duke of Northumberland, his son and Lady Jane Grey were in the Tower and convicted of high treason. Within weeks all three had been executed.

John Huddlestone started rebuilding Sawston Hall almost immediately. When Mary married King Philip of Spain the following year she appointed John to an important position. For a few years John Huddlestone held a position of honour, a respected Catholic under a Catholic Queen.

X X X

When Mary's short reign came to an end in 1558 with her death, the situation changed. Huddlestone lost his job as Vice-chamberlain to King Philip. As soon as he heard that Protestant Elizabeth was to be Queen, John decided to add a priest's hole to the house, just in case. These were little hidden rooms where Catholic priests could hide if anyone came to search for them.

He consulted his priest who recommended a very good carpenter, trustworthy and skilled. This man, called Nicholas, had learnt his trade from his father, and had begun to specialize in these secret hidey-holes. He did the work all himself, in both wood and stone, so none of the local servants could know where the holes were, in case they gave the secret away.

For Sawston Hall they decided to build several holes, knowing they would probably need them. They put some tiny rooms in the attic, one off the main bedroom, one under the staircase, and one in the tower. And for all we know, they put in more, but they have not yet been discovered.

The tower room was one of the most comfortable. The tower itself, directly above the chapel where the priest would spend a great deal of his time, had a stone staircase. The wooden ceiling tiles were held in by wooden pegs, and Nicholas worked hard carving wooden pegs and pretending to be simply repairing the ceiling. In fact, he was cunningly building a priest's hole, complete with potty-style toilet, under the floorboards of the landing. When it was completed, the priest could say prayers in the chapel just below the tower, under the brightly coloured orange ceiling with blue and white rosettes. Then if danger threatened, he could run up the stairs, pull up the floorboards and nip into his hole. Supplied with food and drink by the Huddlestone family or by John Rigby, the steward of the estate who was the only servant who knew the secret, he could stay there until the coast was clear.

In 1585 an Act of Parliament was passed by the Protestant Elizabeth I's government, making it high treason to give food or shelter to any Catholic priest. With the help of their priest's holes, the Huddlestone family continued to practise their religion and to offer safe shelter to priests. Perhaps the ghost of Mary Tudor walks the gallery to this day because she always felt at home there.

The last Huddlestone only left Sawston Hall in the 1980s. The ghost usually appears in the long gallery and in one of the bedrooms. The priest's hole you can still see is in the tower, just above the chapel. It is beneath the floorboards, but you would never find it unless someone shows you.

The holes are thought to have been built by Nicholas Owen, servant to the Jesuit Father Henry Garnet, who constructed hiding places in many Catholic houses throughout the country, for instance in Harvington Hall in Worcester. He left no list of his work, and died under torture in March 1606 without revealing the whereabouts of any of his secret rooms.

Sawston Hall, now the Cambridge Centre for Language Studies (01223 835 099), is in the village of Sawston (on the A505 near Junction 10 of the M11), down Church Lane, opposite the War Memorial. It is best to write or phone for permission before visiting.

CORNWALL

THE MUSICAL MERMAID: ZENNOR

Matthew Trewhella was the best singer in the village of Zennor. He sang in the church choir, and people came from miles around to hear him, so beautiful was his voice. He was a fisherman by trade, and as he walked along the beach to his boat he would practise his songs. Even the seagulls seemed to stop their cries and listen to him. One day, though he did not realize it at the time, someone else far out at sea heard the beautiful music, and swam closer to shore to listen.

The next Sunday a stranger in a long trailing dress of rare greenish-blue material came to church and sat in the back row. No one knew who she was, but she glided gracefully in and sat quietly at the back throughout the service, winding a lock of her long blonde hair about her fingers.

From that day, the lady came often. Soon Matthew became friendly with her, for he was a handsome young man, and she was a beautiful woman. She began to attend the choir practices too. After practice Matthew would walk her part of the way home, but she always left him when they reached the beach near Pendour Cove.

Then one day, Matthew failed to turn up at choir practice. His friends sought him high and low but in vain, and though some said they heard his voice singing far out at sea as they walked along the beach, they never saw him again.

x x x

Two or three years later, as Captain Small cast his anchor in the cove, he was astonished to hear a voice calling him.

"Would you move your anchor," said the voice angrily.

"What… where… good gracious," stammered Captain Small. Looking all around he failed to spot the person calling, until suddenly, glancing down into the water, he saw a beautiful mermaid trying to attract his attention. She had long flowing hair and a greenish-blue tail, scales twinkling in the sunlight. Captain Small's jaw fell open.

"You've dropped your anchor right in front of our door," said the mermaid. "We can't get it open and it's ruined the seaweed in the garden."

The Captain just gasped, for in spite of having heard many tales of mermaids, he had never believed in their existence. He looked a little closer, to see if he could really see her tail, or whether it was just imagination. Suddenly he thought he recognized her. Wasn't she the lady who used to come and listen to Matthew's singing?

"This is probably a very stupid question," he said tentatively. "But you don't by any chance know anything about the where-abouts of my nephew, Matthew?"

"Well, of course I do. He's with me," she snapped. "Now will you move that wretched anchor."

"With you? Our Matthew?" gasped Captain Small. The family had never given up hope of finding him, but this was a bit much.

"Yes, my husband, Matthew," said the mermaid impatiently. "Now for goodness' sake!"

"I... I'm so sorry," Captain Small swallowed, and gave the order to pull up the offending anchor. "Please, give him our regards. Tell him — "

"Don't worry," said the mermaid. "He is well, and happy." And with that and a flip of her strong green tail, she disappeared once more beneath the waves.

Captain Small, completely dazed, returned to shore.

On a warm summer's evening in Zennor Head, by Pendour Cove, if you sit quietly and listen, you may hear Matthew and his mermaid singing together.

You can see the mermaid carved on a bench-end in St Senara, village church of Zennor, around five miles from St Ives on the B3306. The carving dates from the 15th century and holds a mirror in one hand and a comb in the other.

COUNTY DURHAM

THE LAMBTON WORM: FATFIELD

12TH CENTURY (?)

Simon, the heir to Lambton Castle, was a wild boy who never paid attention to his lessons or his elders. He liked only to play with the local boys from the village, and their games were rough and annoyed other people. They went joyriding with carts and donkeys, they stole apples from the trees, they frightened younger children. They liked to go hunting for rabbits and fishing for eels in the local river. The lord of the manor, Simon's father, thought his son should behave better since one day he would be in charge. Simon could not be bothered.

One Sunday, when he should have been in church, Simon

played truant with Stephen, his friend, and two other boys from the village, and went fishing in the river Wear. After hours of dull waiting, chatting and eating their picnic, Simon caught a strange-looking animal. It did not look like the regular eels and small fish they usually caught. It was no longer than his finger, dark green and with two little fins on its back. Its skin was rough and scaly, and it had four short legs, with sharp clawed feet. Its face was repellent, with a long pointed snout, twelve little teeth sharp as pins, and red glowing eyes.

Stephen peered over Simon's shoulder at the animal. "Yuk, throw it back," he advised. But Simon had caught nothing else, and he was intrigued by the little beast. He put it in his pouch. As the boys walked home, kicking stones and chatting, they noticed a foul smell. It came from Simon's pouch. They were just passing the well by the castle, so Simon tossed the squirming worm in, and promptly forgot all about it.

X X X

When Simon was eighteen he went off to fight abroad in the crusades. His father was pleased, for he thought it would be the making of him. Travel, responsibility and hard fighting would be a good experience for his boisterous son.

In Simon's absence, however, the beast in the well continued to grow and grow. Some people commented that when they dropped their buckets in to draw water they heard strange sloshing and gurgling sounds. Eventually the beast became too large for the well, and one night it slithered right out. It immediately ate an old farmer and his dog, returning from a drinking session at the local tavern. They were tasty, especially the farmer who was flavoured with cider. This was just the beginning.

Well fed on local people and cattle, the worm continued to grow. Soon it was long enough to sleep coiled three times around Lambton Hill, which was renamed Worm Hill, a name by which it is still known. Its favourite method of attack was to wrap itself around its prey and squeeze until there was no breath left in the victim. Then it could devour its meal at its leisure. If it could not find anyone when it felt hungry, it would wrap its coils around the nearest tree and hissing with rage would pull up the tree, roots and all. The lord of the manor organized hunting expeditions to try and kill it and teams of men, armed to the teeth, would set out and attack the beast. By now it was so large that a mere stab with a dagger or sword simply enraged it. Moreover if anyone managed to cut a piece off the worm, it simply joined up again! Even if the attackers managed to cut it into two, the halves simply rejoined and the worm seemed even stronger than before. The worm was invincible, no one could defeat it, and many had lost their lives in the attempt. Soon, no one tried any more.

Seven years later, Simon returned from the crusades. It was immediately clear to him that there was a terrible problem, for the countryside was half deserted, the people and the cattle looked terrified, and every so often he came across a tree pulled up by its roots.

"Father, what has happened to your land?" asked Simon as soon as the first greetings were over. The lord of the manor shook his head sadly and described the problem. Simon was struck with remorse, for he instantly recognized the description of his little worm many times magnified, both in appearance and in smell. It was clearly his duty to deal with the disaster he had caused.

First he consulted a local witch. She advised him to stick razors all over his armour and then lure the worm to fight him in the middle of the river. "Only in this way will you defeat the animal," she cackled. "But the price of this advice," she added, "is that you must promise to kill the first creature to greet you after your victory. Otherwise terrible things will befall you and your family."

Simon agreed. He and his father arranged to release a chicken which would be the first creature to greet Simon after the battle.

Simon did not quite see why he should stick razors all over his armour but, as his old friend Stephen pointed out, the witch had a very good reputation for solving problems, so he decided to take her advice. The local blacksmith helped him to weld on the sharp razors.

"If you'd done what I told you years ago," said Stephen snappily (for he had lost several cows the week before to the worm), "and thrown it back in the river, none of this would have happened."

"I know. I'm very sorry," said Simon. "But I am trying to sort it out."

As soon as the armour was ready, Simon rode with Stephen to Worm Hill and shouted defiance at the worm. "Come and get me," he called. "Dinner time!"

Stephen mounted his horse hurriedly and rode away to a safe distance to watch. The worm uncoiled itself at great speed from the hill and hurled itself hungrily at Simon. Simon backed away towards the river until he stood knee-deep in the water. "Come on," he taunted. "Aren't you hungry today?" The worm attacked, but as it tried to crush him by its usual methods, the razors gradually cut into its body. The harder it squeezed, the deeper the blades bit, and as pieces fell from the beast, they were swept away by the river before they could join together again.

Finally Simon got an arm free, and struck the beast's ugly head free from its body. With a last furious hiss, the head floated downstream and the rest of the animal expired. Simon signalled joyfully to his father with a bugle call, and Stephen shouted happily from his look-out.

But then disaster struck. In his excitement at hearing the triumphant bugle Simon's father ran down as fast as he could towards the river. He completely forgot to release the chicken as they had arranged. Simon, who had also forgotten the witch's advice in the excitement, suddenly recalled his bargain and stood in dismay as his father approached.

"Father, no, no!" he cried. "Go back, go back!"

But it was too late. The old lord was at his side, embracing him, congratulating him.

"Well done, my boy, well done. What a fight!"

Simon stood in silence. Stephen, aghast, said to him, "Simon, no, you can't kill your own father!" but he need not have worried. Despite his fear of the witch's curse, Simon was unable to kill the first living creature he met, his proud father.

But the witch's prediction came true. His failure to keep his promise had terrible consequences, for a curse did indeed fall on the family. For nine generations, no Lambton was to die in his own bed. Sickness and battle claimed them, and a quiet old age was denied to all Lambtons.

Worm Hill near Fatfield, just south of Washington, off the A1(M) in County Durham, is on the north bank of the Wear, 1.5 miles from Lambton Hall. Worm Well is between the hill and the river Wear.

The Hill is currently vacant...

CUMBRIA

THE MYSTERIOUS KNIGHT: ST BEES

1981/1370

One day in 1981, an archaeologist arrived at St Bees Priory, a church on the coast of Cumbria. Her name was Deirdre O'Sullivan and she had come to investigate what lay beneath the soil around the church. By the time she had spent several rain-sodden days trying to get her spade into the earth in the freezing cold and wet, she was ready for a new idea. It came from a gentleman she had met while preparing to start work, John Todd. He lived and worked in the area and had become very interested in the history of this old church.

"Why don't you try in here, right inside the church," he suggested. "As far as I know it's never been investigated. You could get special permission." It was under cover and out of the rain, so Deirdre promptly agreed, although without much enthusiasm. However, she had given up the chance of a holiday in Italy for this, and had to have something to show for the time she had wasted so far.

For three days she grimly removed layers of earth and piled them neatly at the side of her trench. Every day John Todd came by and asked her how she was doing. Every day she answered politely, "Fine, thank you," and felt like murdering him as she watched him walk away to his nice warm house. Each evening she left the church and walked out into the pouring rain, back to her bed and breakfast, wondering why she was bothering.

Then on the third afternoon, as she shovelled away yet another bucketful of earth, she suddenly noticed something. There were small traces of iron, and soon the shape of a wooden box with iron bands holding it began to appear. It was a large box, shaped like a coffin, but it seemed somehow unusual. Deirdre scraped away for the rest of the day.

The next morning she looked forward to John Todd's arrival. By now she had almost finished uncovering the box and she and John knelt down to open it very, very carefully. Inside was clay packing. They removed this. Then came a lead covering, dark and hard, and shaped like a body. Deirdre and John looked at one another. Only another skeleton, they thought with disappointment. But they were wrong. Archaeologists find skeletons all the time, but they are usually just a pile of bones which can tell you very little. This one was special.

"Look," said Deirdre excitedly. She knelt down and showed

John the crack at the side of the covering. Together they opened up the lead shell, and lifted off the top. Inside lay the fresh-looking body of a man, wrapped neatly in cloth and string. On the body's chest lay a long hank of what looked like a woman's hair.

John Todd and Deirdre O'Sullivan looked at one another in puzzlement. How had the body been preserved so that it looked as though the man had died yesterday? And who was he? There was no name on the coffin. And what was the woman's hair doing there? Was it a long-lost love of his who had cut her locks for love of him when he died? And how had he died? He was not that old, and had clearly died a violent death. All these questions needed answers. But what should they do first? They could not just leave a fresh body lying around in the church. That was when they decided to ring the police.

Sergeant Cobb arrived at the same time as the ambulance. The body was quickly taken to the local hospital while Sergeant Cobb pulled out his notebook to question Deirdre and John.

"So, where did you find the body?" he began pompously.

"In the church," said Deirdre.

"I see." Sergeant Cobb wrote slowly. "And do you know who it might be?"

"No." The policeman frowned and wrote: "Murder victim unknown."

"Hmm, so when do you think he died?"

"Maybe five hundred years ago?"

Sergeant Cobb looked up sharply from his notebook. "Are you trying to be funny, miss?" he asked sternly.

"No, no," Deirdre hastened to assure him.

"Well, hmm." He looked back at his notebook. There were certain questions you had to ask when you found a body. Such as, who in the family should we tell about his death? And, how did he die? But to all of these questions Deirdre and John shook their heads. They just did not know yet.

This was the first case of murder Sergeant Cobb had had to deal with, and it was not going the way he had been taught in police training school.

x x x

Over the following months John Todd and Deirdre O'Sullivan managed to piece together part of the story of the unknown body.

He had been buried in an important position in the church, so he was probably a knight of some importance locally, but why had his burial place not been marked, either on the grave or in the parish records? He was probably a knight, and the closest guess they could make was a local lord called Sir Anthony de Lucy for whose death they could find no other record. Sir Anthony, they discovered, had gone off in 1367 with fifteen horsemen to fight with the Teutonic Knights against the heathens on the frontiers of Russia.

The Teutonic Knights were a religious organization of young men from good, rich families, and this perfectly fitted Sir Anthony's background. They vowed to be poor, chaste and obedient, to take care of the sick, and to fight the enemies of the church. They wore black clothes under a white cloak with a black cross on the left shoulder. They ate plain food and prayed frequently. They were only allowed plain armour and had to bring three or four good horses to last them for a whole battle.

The St Bees knight had had short hair, just beginning to go a little grey, and a beard. He had a very sore tooth, and must have had toothache all the time, which may have meant he could not concentrate properly on his fighting. The police surgeon said he had died from a deep chest wound which had penetrated the lung, possibly while he was on horseback, so probably in battle or fighting a tournament.

It was known that if a Teutonic Knight was killed fighting far from home, his friends would try to arrange for the body to be properly wrapped up, so it would survive the journey, and be sent home. It all fitted the mysterious pattern. But had he died in disgrace to be buried so secretly?

And whose was the mysterious hair laid on his chest after his death? Did the unknown girl wait years for him, and then when she saw his body brought home lifeless, cut off all her hair and lay it on his body before killing herself or perhaps entering a nunnery?

Who knows?

There is a display in the church with photos of the archaeological dig and the St Bees Man. Dr John Todd has presented the story of the discovery of the St Bees Man to various universities. Deirdre O'Sullivan is still working on further aspects of the mystery.

St Bees is south of Whitehaven on the west coast of Britain.

CUMBRIA

THE DEVIL'S BRIDGE:
KIRKBY LONSDALE

MIDDLE AGES

Mother Jennifer was a crafty old lady who lived in Yorkshire and used to come into the town of Kirkby Lonsdale every Tuesday to sell her eggs at the local market. She would rise specially early that morning, and with her little fat dog, Charlie, she would make the rounds of her hens and collect the fresh brown eggs. She would pack them carefully in a basket, whistle to Charlie and set off. Charlie had problems keeping up, for his legs were so short they hardly touched the ground.

She had to cross the river Lune to get to town and in dry

weather when the water was shallow it could be forded easily. In winter, when the river was in spate, she had to walk all the way round, and use a bridge in the next village, but this added many extra miles to her trip. So all through the summer she would simply wade across the river, hoicking her dress up around her knees and calling to Charlie to follow her. He never did – he hated to get wet, so she always had to put down her basket and wade back to fetch him. And of course, he did not want to be caught, because he was very worried about being carried across. He was always sure that one day she would drop him in. So he would run away, and she would have to chase him, and then carry him squirming across the river.

"One of these days, Charlie," she scolded, "I will drop you in, wriggling around like that."

At the other bank she would put him down, and in great relief he would give himself a shake and run ahead, looking like a fat doughnut on little stumpy legs. This happened every Tuesday.

But one day, in early autumn, although it had started off sunny, the weather soon took a turn for the worse. By the time Mother Jennifer and Charlie had arrived at the market and set up the stall, a few drops of rain had begun to fall. As the sky grew darker and the rain grew harder, the few people who were out shopping went home.

"You know what, Charlie," said Mother Jennifer. "Let's go home. This is a waste of time, and I'm wet through."

Charlie nodded in agreement, and sneezed sadly. He had crawled under the stall to shelter from the rain, but there was a cold wind under the table and he too was very fed up.

They set off home, but they were in for a nasty shock. By the time they reached the river it was in full spate. That morning they had waded across as usual, but now the current flowed deep, angry and strong. There was no way that Mother Jennifer could get across herself, let alone carrying a reluctant dog.

"What are we going to do, Charlie?" asked Mother Jennifer in despair. She was cold and tired, and when she thought of her nice little cottage with a warm fire and a cup of something hot, she felt like crying. "Oh, I'd do anything to be on the other side."

There was a clap of thunder and the lightning flashed. Charlie cowered against the back of Mother Jennifer's calves and pretended he was somewhere else.

"Good afternoon," said a polite voice. "I believe you called?" A tall elegant gentleman dressed in black, with a silken cloak hanging from his shoulders, bowed gracefully to Mother Jennifer. The old lady sniffed miserably and looked silently at him.

"Shall I help you to the other side of the river?" he asked.

Wild thoughts of the elegant gentleman giving her a piggyback or finding her a small boat chased through Mother Jennifer's mind. "Oh, yes please," she answered.

"But do you agree to the conditions? I will build you a bridge but the first living soul to cross will be mine." Mother Jennifer was nodding as she searched in her basket for a tissue to wipe her streaming nose. When the explanation sunk in she could have cried with vexation. He was going to build her a bridge! A fat lot of use that was going to be. It surely would not be ready for months, and she had so hoped to get home by evening.

But the gentleman had taken her nod as an agreement. He lifted his cloak, rose in the air and flew off to get some rocks and start building. Before the astonished eyes of Mother Jennifer and the cowering Charlie, the gentleman flew backwards and forwards bringing in the material for a substantial bridge. In no time at all, he had built the two side spans of the bridge, and apart from a mishap up on Casterton Fell where he tripped over his cloak and dropped a load of rocks, the bridge was nearly finished. Soon three great arches spanned the river, and Mother Jennifer could cross in safety. The elegant gentleman, a little out of breath, stood in the centre, smiling in a friendly fashion.

But Mother Jennifer was a crafty old lady, and she realized

there was something strange about this gentleman. After all, it was not every day you met a strange man dressed in black, who flew around being helpful. She thought hard to remember exactly what he had said before he agreed to build the bridge. Then, reaching into her ample basket, she pulled out a little bun she had saved from lunch. She threw it across the river. Charlie, who had been hidden by Mother Jennifer's skirts, smelt food and rushed to eat the bun. In spite of his short legs, when it came to food he could move extremely fast. He galloped across the bridge, tongue hanging out in excitement.

The gentleman's brows snapped together in anger. He did not want an overfed little dog's soul – he had wanted Mother Jennifer's. She stood there with bated breath, for she loved Charlie in spite of his annoying ways, and the elegant gentleman did look very annoyed. Then suddenly he grinned ruefully at the cunning old lady, and disappeared in a puff of smoke. Charlie, mouth full of bun, waited wagging his tail on the far side, and Mother Jennifer picked up her basket and crossed the new bridge.

The three-arched Devil's Bridge at Kirkby Lonsdale probably dates from the early Middle Ages. At any rate, it needed repairing in 1365, according to the earliest documentary evidence which mentions a grant made to Richard de Wisbeche, a vicar of Kirkby Lonsdale, to charge a toll to fund the repairs. Devil's Bridge has been pedestrians only since 1932.

You can see a fall of rock up on Casterton Fell.

Kirkby Lonsdale is a quick drive from the M6, and Casterton and High Casterton are nearby on the A683.

DEVON

SAND PACKAGES:
WOOLACOMBE SANDS

1170

Sir William de Tracy looked up in despair and cried, "More rope, quick, more rope!" As the wind rose and the waves pounded on the beach, he found it almost impossible to tie up millions of grains of sand into orderly parcels. However much rope he used, the sand trickled through and left him with knots of rope, and only a few grains of sand remained within the parcel. It was worst on days like today, when the wind blew and the sea was rough. On sunny, calm days he could wrap quite a few parcels of damp sand, and they stayed neat – but even then only until the sand dried out, or the tide rose and washed his work away. Looking out over the miles of dunes that covered the beach at Woolacombe, Sir William realized he still had many centuries of work to do. But that was just punishment for the terrible crime he had committed...

X X X

Sir William de Tracy was working in the household of Thomas à Becket when Thomas was appointed Archbishop of Canterbury, the highest position in the English Church. Thomas à Becket was the King's best friend, and everyone thought that the new Archbishop and Henry II would continue as friends. However, no sooner had Thomas accepted the job than he began to take it seriously. He had been the most frivolous courtier, but now he got rid of all his fashionable clothes, gave away his rich furniture and paintings, stopped playing chess and dice, and no longer hunted with his dogs or his falcons. King Henry simply could not understand such behaviour.

"Come on, let's go drinking," he cried.

"Your Majesty," Thomas replied seriously, "it is no longer suitable for me to behave in such a manner. I am now head of the church. I must set a good example. I'm sorry."

King Henry was very disgruntled, for drinking alone or hunting alone was not as much fun as it had been with Thomas. Sir William de Tracy and other knights left the Archbishop's household and joined the king, but somehow it was still not the same. The King began to feel hostile towards his one-time friend.

The Archbishop, meanwhile, had completely changed his way of life. Every day he rose before dawn, went to the door of his palace and invited in all the poor who had gathered there. He brought them in for breakfast, and gave them money and clothes. Each day he held a feast for one hundred poor people.

When Henry asked for advice with problems of the kingdom, Thomas wrote back to the King that he was too busy with the work of the Church and could no longer help Henry with the government of the realm. Henry was furious.

X X X

During the next few years the King and his old friend clashed over many subjects. For instance, King Henry wanted to appoint his own friends as bishops. Thomas à Becket refused.

"Your Majesty, it is not for you to choose the bishops. It is for me and the Pope in Rome."

When King Henry realized that Thomas was blocking his wishes in such an important matter, he exploded. He was feared for his terrible temper and the courtiers backed away in terror. Sometimes when he was really annoyed Henry would tear down the curtains and rip them up, or lie on the floor drumming his heels and chewing at the rugs, so uncontrolled were his rages. This time King Henry hurled his goblet to the floor and shouted, "Is there not one among you who will avenge my honour and rid me of this turbulent priest?"

Sir William de Tracy looked around and caught the eye of three other knights, Reginald Fitz-Urse, Hugh de Moreville and Richard Le Breton. He could see they were thinking the way he was – that King Henry would be delighted if Archbishop Thomas à Becket were removed from the scene. It would be a big favour for the king and he would doubtless reward them well. Why, he had virtually ordered it.

It was Christmas Eve but the four knights met secretly later that night, and decided to set off for Canterbury at daybreak.

X X X

Thomas had heard rumours that a party of soldiers was coming to kill him, but he had decided not to try and escape. He would stay and face whatever was coming.

There was a loud hammering on the door of his apartments. His friends, clerks and monks, begged him at least to take refuge in the church, which he could reach through the cloister. Seeing their concern, Thomas agreed, saying, "Since it is the hour for my prayers anyway, I shall go to the church."

Once he was inside, the monks started to bolt the door with a huge iron bar, but Thomas said, "This is a church, not a fortress." He lifted the bar out of the way.

He went further into the church, and was climbing the steps towards the choir when he heard the clashing of weapons and loud threatening voices. He could still have escaped, either by hiding in the crypt or creeping up a hidden staircase, but he chose to stay where he was, leaning against a pillar by the altar.

"Don't move, anyone," one of the four knights shouted as they rushed into the church, swords drawn and in full armour.

"Where is the traitor?" cried Reginald Fitz-Urse. There was no answer. Thomas was not going to respond to that name.

"Where is the Archbishop?" Reginald conceded the point.

"Here I am," Thomas called out. "Why have you come armed into the house of God? What do you intend?"

"To kill you!"

"I am ready to die for God. But don't hurt any of my friends."

The four knights had surrounded the Archbishop, but they were reluctant to kill him within the church. It would be a terrible crime. Sir William de Tracy caught hold of Thomas and started to try and drag him out of church. But before becoming Archbishop, Thomas had been a keen horse-rider and a good soldier, and he was still strong. He resisted, and tore Sir William's surcoat at the neck. Sir William struck him with the blunt side of his sword and shouted "Run or you will die!" for the knights were still hesitating about killing him at the foot of the altar.

But Thomas refused to move. He started to pray, and the knights had no choice, but to attack right there, in that holiest of places.

The priests and monks who had entered the church with

Thomas were hiding under the chairs and behind pillars. Only one, Edward Grim, came forward to help, but as Sir William aimed the first sword blow at Thomas, Edward was badly injured in the arm. He fell to the side, and then the four knights rained blows on the Archbishop. At first Thomas stood leaning on the pillar, but soon he slumped to the floor.

When the deed was done and the Archbishop dead, the murderers escaped to his palace. There they broke open Thomas's chests and desks, and stole his gold chalice, a ring with a beautiful sapphire and a priceless jewelled knife which he had kept from the old days when he was a courtier. On the way out they rifled through his documents and removed anything that looked interesting. Then they rode away taking his horses.

X X X

In the church, the monks and clerks stared in horror at what had been done. Crowds gathered and people began to weep, for the Archbishop had been very popular. Meanwhile the four knights returned to the castle of Saltwood and sat down for a meal. It was hungry work, riding and murdering.

It was only then that they began to realize what they had done. The servants looked terrified and many left the castle that night on some pretext. The dogs skulked under the table, and refused to take food from the hands of the four knights. The King sent no message of congratulations.

In fact, King Henry was horrified at what had happened. He had meant them to kill Thomas à Becket, but not in church, and not in such a horrible and public way. And he was surprised at how upset his people were. He shut himself up alone for three days, seeing no one and eating almost nothing.

The knights stayed at home for a whole year, and no one visited them, but after that time three of them quietly returned to court. Only William de Tracy still stayed at home. The following year, 1172, Thomas was made a saint and the King went on pilgrimage, his bare feet bleeding, tears streaming from his eyes, to pray at Thomas's grave. As the months passed, those who visited the shrine or prayed to St Thomas experienced many miracles. Their diseases were cured, their loved ones returned. But Edward Grim, whose arm had been hurt in the struggle in the church, continued to suffer. For a year after the injury, the doctors could not set his arm. Then one night, as though in a dream, Thomas à Becket came into the room, laid a wet linen cloth on the arm, and said, "Go, you are healed." And in the morning Edward's arm was indeed healed.

X X X

William de Tracy was still at home. Every time he learned of another miracle performed at the grave of the man he had murdered, he grew more depressed.

"I wish I were dead," he said to himself. "I wish the earth would just open and swallow me up."

Life was so unbearable at home where no one would speak to him except his favourite daughter, Matilda, that he moved to a huge cavern by the sea called Crookhorn. There was only one way to reach this cavern, and that was by scrambling over some dark rocks west of Ilfracombe, and you could only get there at low tide. In fact, during most of the year, the cavern was completely full of water, and it was in this miserable spot that William lay and thought bitterly about his crime. Once a day, Matilda climbed around the rocks and brought him some food. One day she brought him a letter.

"A messenger brought this," she told him, as she unwrapped her bundle. "He said his name was Edward Grim, and you would remember him because you hurt his arm."

Sir William de Tracy sat up, his face completely pale in the dark. "Yes," he whispered. "I remember him."

Matilda laid out some bread and cheese on a clean cloth for her father. "He said to tell you that when Thomas came and cured his arm, he brought you this letter at the same time. Here, have some of this ham, it's delicious."

She passed him a platter with food, but he ignored it and picked up the letter with a shaking hand. Matilda glanced at his face and was shocked at the expression.

"Father," Matilda gasped. "Do you think he means that Archbishop Thomas à Becket came back from the dead and cured his arm?"

After he had read the letter, Sir William dropped his head in his hands. "I must make bundles of sand, and tie them up in parcels on Woolacombe Sands, until my crime is forgotten," he groaned.

x x x

And there Sir William groans and labours still, in the golden sands of Woolacombe, and when the wind blows and the surf pounds, he groans louder as his parcels are scattered abroad. But when he sees people building sandcastles he is happier, for a well-built sandcastle is easier to wrap.

Thomas à Becket was murdered on 29th December 1170 in what is now Canterbury Cathedral. The sands at Woolacombe are still predominantly untied. If you go up to Baggy Point you can apparently hear Sir William mournfully crying, "More rope." Crookhorn cavern has now gone; it has been washed away.

There is a rumour that Sir William spent some time near an old farmhouse now called Woolacombe Tracy.

Woolacombe is a few miles west of Ilfracombe, opposite Lundy Island, on the B3231/B3343.

DEVON

THE ARMADA SHIP
THAT CAME BACK FOR MORE:
BOLT TAIL

1588

By 1586 King Philip of Spain had had enough. Queen Elizabeth of England, to whose sister Mary he had once been married before her untimely death, kept encouraging her captains to attack his ships. His treasure, travelling from America to Spain, had been captured, his ships kidnapped and refitted with English flags. It was unacceptable. What's more, the Pope had decreed that America belonged to the Spanish, so the English – nasty little Protestant country – had no right to be there in the first place. So thought King Philip.

But the English did not give a fig for the Pope any more, nor for the Spanish king, and they sailed wherever they wanted.

As news came in of yet another Spanish ship captured on the high seas, of another Spanish town burnt by the English, Philip grew more and more determined to teach them a lesson. He forgot that his men had killed English sailors in Mexico, after promising them safety. He forgot that he had refused English ships permission to enter Spanish ports even when there was a dangerous storm. He even forgot that his ambassador had just been caught plotting to murder Queen Elizabeth. He only thought how he would like to teach those English pirates a lesson, how he would like to get rid of Queen Elizabeth who did not respect the Pope, and above all how he should really like to be King of England. An invasion was the only solution.

He summoned Don Alonso Perez de Guzman, Duke of Medina Sidonia, and appointed him Captain General of the invasion fleet, the huge Armada. 9,000 sailors and 19,000 soldiers were packed into 130 ships. They had 2,431 guns on board. But the Duke did not want the job. 'I am always seasick,' he wrote to the King, begging to be excused. 'I don't know anything about navigation or sea fighting.' The King said that was tough luck, he was going to remain in charge of the Armada, whether he liked it or not.

One of the ships was the *San Pedro Mayor*. It was a large ship, and it was supposed to serve as a hospital if anyone was sick or injured. It held 100 soldiers and another 50 men to take care of the sick. They loaded water, food, bandages and medicine and waited excitedly for the rest of the ships to get ready. The most excited person on board was Diego, the cabin boy, the least important crew member. His job was to clean out the officers' cabins, help with the laundry and carry out small errands.

In May 1588 the huge fleet set off from the Spanish coast to attack England, but was immediately swept out to sea by a storm. It took two weeks for the ships to get back to where they had started, while some of the smaller ships were blown even further away and could not return. Diego, and many others, thought it was a very bad start.

At last the fleet set off properly. It arrived off Cornwall in July and started to sail down the English Channel. When Sir Francis Drake was told of their arrival, he was playing bowls at Plymouth and refused to cut his game short. "There is time to finish the game and beat the Spanish afterwards," he said. Later he joined his crew on board his ship. The English ships began to gather in front of and behind the Spanish Armada, but they waited for a good opportunity and just shadowed the Spaniards for the moment.

As the crew of the *San Pedro Mayor* watched the English coast go by, Diego suddenly spotted a boy about his own age on a high cliff, watching the fleet. On an impulse, he waved. The boy, whose name was Thomas Aske, and who had whistled for his dog Huw and run out to watch the ships, waved back, though he should not have really because the Spaniards were the enemy. He lived near Hope Cove, under the shadow of the big cliffs at Bolt Tail, and he had come up to watch the invasion. Maybe the Spaniards were human after all, he thought. That boy looked like he might be all right. They were not to know they would meet a few months later, in very different circumstances.

Diego was called back to work. Thomas watched until both the Spanish and the English ships were out of sight, and then rushed home to report to his father what he had seen.

The Spanish fleet continued through the Channel. Suddenly, the *San Salvador*, which was one of the largest ships and carried most of the money to pay the soldiers, exploded. No one knew why. When two other ships came to rescue the men, they collided, damaging both ships. It was another dreadful omen.

The rest of the huge Armada continued all the way round the south coast of England, and off Calais, near Gravelines, Drake and Sir John Hawkins, another much-feared English captain, were finally ready to attack them. They launched burning fire ships into the midst of the fleet, and in the confusion sank three huge galleons, and damaged many more. No English ships were lost and only one junior captain was killed. But in the Spanish fleet, the story was very different. Most of the ships were damaged, many were injured, and no one felt like continuing to fight.

But how to get home? What was left of the Armada knew it would never be allowed through the English Channel twice. The weather and the currents were also now against them, so the only way back to Spain was to go all the way round the north of Scotland. This was very dangerous, since they were all so tired and upset, their ships were damaged, and the weather was terrible. By now Diego was desperate to return home.

It took them weeks to travel round the dangerous, rocky shores of Scotland and Ireland. At least 26 ships were wrecked, and they grew sick and weary of looking for their colleagues. In the end Diego's ship, the *San Pedro Mayor*, was travelling all alone, having lost her companion ships. No one knew if the others had been sunk or just gone home by a different route. In the fog, the wind and the rain, no one knew anything any more, except that they wanted to be back home.

After weeks of sailing, when they were all so tired they could no longer bear the sight of one another, Diego escaped from his work and was looking out at the shore again, wondering how much further they would have to sail. The cliffs looked vaguely familiar, and suddenly on the crest, he thought he saw the same boy he had seen all those weeks ago, with his dog. Surely it could not be the same place? That would mean that the captain had made a terrible mistake. Instead of continuing south when they had rounded Ireland, they had continued to keep close to land, and had come round the whole country again. They were back in the English channel again, off Devon. What a disaster!

Diego could see the English boy frantically waving now. Had he too recognized the ship, the only Spanish ship, surely, stupid enough to come round enemy waters twice? Diego waved back, but the boy was gesturing frantically at the rocks below the cliff. It almost looked as if he were trying to warn them about something. Beside the boy his big black dog jumped and barked, infected by his master's excitement. Suddenly with an awful thud where his stomach had been, Diego realized they were driving straight for the cliffs. He ran to the front of the ship, where the helmsman had obviously fallen asleep with weariness and failed to notice the danger. Diego rang the alarm and called all the men to come up on deck.

On the cliffs, Thomas Aske could only watch helplessly as the gallant *San Pedro Mayor*, who had taken her crew safely all the way round the north coasts of Scotland and Ireland, through the bitterest storms, headed straight onto the rocks and tore out her bottom under the Bolt Tail cliffs. As Thomas started to run back down to the village to raise the alarm, he heard the dreadful crunch of timber on rock. If only he could save that Spanish boy whom he somehow regarded as a friend. He had seen the shock and fear in the boy's gestures as he realized what Thomas was trying to tell him.

The villagers, Thomas's father included, rushed to launch their rowing boats and save the men from the wreck. Luckily the huge ship settled slowly and most were saved and brought back to land. Thomas, anxiously watching on the beach was delighted to see a small frightened face among the first to be rescued. The two boys embraced, and no words were necessary – luckily, since neither spoke the other's language. Huw leapt up and down and licked whichever ear he could reach.

Diego stayed with Thomas and his family, where he was allowed to rest and eat his fill until he could be sent back home. Meanwhile the officers were taken to the nearby town of Kingsbridge to be held until they could be ransomed by their families, and there they bemoaned their fate and tried to understand how they could possibly have been so unlucky as to have gone round the country twice.

Bolt Tail lies east of Bigbury Bay, 15 miles beyond Plymouth by sea. Leave the A379 at Kingsbridge, or walk following the cliff-top path up Bolt Head from Salcombe. You can drop into Hope Cove over the Tail.

The San Pedro Mayor was shipwrecked on October 28th 1588. In reward for his services, Sir Francis Drake was given (among many other gifts) the manor of Stancombe, near Kingsbridge.

Only one third of the Armada got back to Spain: out of nine thousand seamen and nineteen thousand soldiers, twenty thousand died.

DORSET

THE CERNE ABBAS GIANT

C. AD 500

There once was a fierce giant who lived in Dorset. His friends called him Helith, but he had very few, because giants of this type are not very sociable. He was 60 metres tall, as high as a six-storey building, and he carried a huge club 40 metres long, the size of a large tree, in his right hand. He used this club to hit his food on the head – sheep, people, cows... Hardly surprising that everyone was terrified, and as soon as people heard his heavy footsteps they would run and hide.

One day David Penfold, a young shepherd, was taking his flock to graze on a nearby hillside called Trundle when he heard the dreaded footsteps. There was no time to rescue the whole flock, though he hurried them along as fast as they would go. However, he managed to save most of the sheep and hid with them in a grove of trees, trying to muffle their bleating, and listening in terror and outrage to the sound of Helith making a good meal of the stragglers.

When he had finished his lunch, the giant took a long drink at the stream at the bottom of the hill, and then set off about his business. But as he climbed the hill, he was suddenly overcome with sleep, and decided to lie down and give his full stomach a rest. Within seconds he was fast asleep.

David saw his chance. He left the sheep grazing quietly and ran as fast as he could down to the village. He rushed up to a group of men standing drinking outside the local inn and shouted, "Quickly, here's our chance. The giant is fast asleep. Let's get him."

The men looked at one another, and then without further ado grasped their scythes and axes or whatever lay to hand, and set off for the hillside. Helith still lay fast asleep, but his right hand grasped his huge club at the ready, and the men hushed one another and began to tiptoe closer.

When the giant was surrounded, David gave the signal. In no time at all, the giant was beheaded, and the men grinned and cheered. After all these years of terror, their problems were solved.

But what would happen if one of Helith's friends decided to move into the area? They decided to cut round the giant's body as it lay in the grass and leave a picture of his outline, there on the hillside, as a warning to all other giants.

The men worked all day, with David guiding and calling instructions. The earth was chalky under the grass, and the shape stood out white against the green hillside. When they had finished and had dragged the giant's body away for disposal, the figure lay huge and menacing. "Let this be a warning to giants to avoid our village," the villagers said. Then they shouldered their scythes, shovels and axes and went back down the hill for a drink.

The Cerne Abbas giant is thought to be over 1500 years old. He lies on the hillside face at Trundle Hill, a quarter of a mile north of Cerne Abbas church.

Cerne Abbas village is on the A352, north of Dorchester.

ESSEX

THE NUN IN THE WALL:
BORLEY RECTORY

1667

Marie Lairre was a laughing girl whose family had forced her to become a nun as a young child. She was happy at first and worked in the convent hospital. There she met Brother William, the herbalist, a monk from the local Borley monastery.

As they worked together, Marie Lairre nursing the sick and Brother William supplying the medicines, they began to fall in love. Soon they had both decided to leave their religious lives and get married.

The local lord, however, whose wife frequently visited the hospital and who had noticed the beautiful nun while accompanying his wife, had other ideas. He wanted Marie Lairre himself, and if he could not have her, no one else should, especially not Brother William. So when Marie Lairre and Brother William applied for permission to leave from their superiors, the lord intervened.

In no time at all, the lovers were parted. Brother William was transferred to a distant monastery. The lord told the Mother Superior, in charge of the convent, that he would burn the building to the ground if his wishes were not followed. And his edict was that Marie Lairre be sentenced to death. In return, he offered to pay for a new wing for the convent. The only chance of escape for the young nun was to agree to go and live with the lord. She refused and her fate was sealed.

Showing no mercy, the lord ordered that Marie Lairre be placed in a small space between the brickwork of the new wing of the convent, while the walls were built up around her. The other nuns were distressed but had no choice. The lord himself stood by and watched as the last brick was set in place. Then he rode off in his coach and four, grimly satisfied.

It was thought by all that that would be the end of the matter.

x x x

A few weeks later, the Mother Superior thought she saw Marie Lairre walking around the cloisters. Then the wicked lord too saw her while galloping past the convent in his coach, and his horses were so frightened they bolted. He fell out and was badly injured. Soon many of the other nuns saw her ghost, and they began to abandon the nunnery.

With the wicked lord dead of his injuries and the nunnery

deserted, Marie Lairre's ghost acquired a carriage drawn by headless horses, a terrible sight. The coach was similar to the one the lord had used before his accident, and she rode around the area in this for several centuries. The local people respected her and she harmed no one.

In 1863, however, the new local rector, the Reverend Bull, built a rectory for his family right across the course of her nightly ride. Marie Lairre was clearly unimpressed. She kept staring at him with a woebegone expression through the window in his study as he tried to write his sermons. He had the window bricked up, and tried to ignore her.

It was difficult. His servants refused to stay with him, because the coach continued to take the same route as it had for many centuries, but since the Reverend Bull's dining room now lay right across her path, she simply galloped through the walls and then across the lawn. She began to appear in the daytime too, though usually without her horses, and the gardener and the postman initially mistook her for a visiting nun.

In 1930 a new vicar, Lionel Foyster, moved in to the rectory with his young wife, Marianne. Marie Lairre began to write to her, scribbling on the walls and begging for light, for candles so she could hold formal prayers, for help. Soon Lionel and Marianne could take no more and moved out.

A journalist called Harry Price leased the empty rectory and carried out many investigations. The house became known in the newspapers as 'the most haunted house in England.' A seance was held, and Marie Lairre announced that the house would burn down that night. Everyone waited, but nothing happened.

A new owner, Captain Gregson, took the lease, not believing all this rubbish about ghosts. But then, one evening, nearly a year after the spirit's promise, Captain Gregson had problems with his two dogs. A spaniel and a setter, they always went out into the garden for a quick visit in the evenings, before settling down for the night. That evening, 27 February 1939, the dogs simply refused to come back in. Captain Gregson shouted at them for a bit, but then, irritated, decided they could stay outside if they were being so obstinate. He went back to the study, and settled down with a book of military memoirs. Suddenly a lamp fell over of its own accord, untouched by human hand.

The rectory burst into flames. Captain Gregson just managed to escape, and as he stood watching his house burn down with his dogs at his side he could see the figure of a nun at the window. No one has built another house on the site of Borley Rectory, but at night people still see Marie Lairre in her coach galloping past.

Marie Lairre is supposed to have died in 1667. Borley Rectory burnt down exactly eleven months after Marie Lairre announced that it would.

The village of Borley lies off the A134 near Sudbury, south of Bury St Edmunds.

GLOUCESTERSHIRE

SPRING SAINT: WINCHCOMBE

821

When King Kenulf died his son Kenelm became King, though he was only seven years old. He was a sweet, good boy, but his older sister Quendreda was very different. She was grown up and thought she ought to be queen, in place of her silly little brother. She plotted against him, and finally asked her lover, Ascobert, to take Kenelm to the forest and get rid of him. Ascobert, a tough ambitious man, agreed, hoping that after the boy's death he could marry Quendreda and become King himself.

"Come, Your Majesty," he said to the child. "The sun is shining, it's a beautiful day to be out hunting in the forest."

Kenelm readily agreed, for he loved the forest, and the two set off. After spending the whole day outside, chasing around the trees, Kenelm was tired and lay down for a rest. Ascobert looked down at him grimly and started to dig a deep hole to serve as the boy's grave.

Kenelm suddenly woke up and said sleepily, "This is not the place for you to kill me." He smiled and stuck a twig in the partly-dug hole. "Look, we'll plant a tree here." And he laughed as the twig grew black buds and dark flowers burst from the small tree.

But Ascobert merely scowled, and abandoned his digging. He picked up their jackets and set off. "We must get back," he said. "Come on, hurry up."

Kenelm skipped along beside him, but as they reached a particularly dense part of the forest, Ascobert turned on the boy and killed him with his hunting knife. As the child fell, a white dove sprang from his chest and flew away.

Ascobert hid the body under a thorn bush and returned in triumph to Quendreda. Unfortunately for him, once he had served his purpose, Quendreda had no more time for Ascobert.

Meanwhile the dove which had flown out of Kenelm's chest flew all the way to Rome, to the Pope, who was praying in St Peter's church. The tired bird dropped a little scroll at his feet, and once it was translated for the Pope he read:

In Clent Cow-pasture under a thorn
Of head bereft lies Kenelm, King born.

The Pope immediately sent a message to Wilfred, Archbishop of Canterbury, who sent out search parties to comb the forests, but the forests were dense and they did not know where to start. They hunted for days in vain, returning empty-handed every evening.

An old lady who had heard about the search came to visit the Archbishop. "My lord," she said, sinking stiffly to her knees.

Wilfred helped her to rise. "My lord, I hear you are searching the forest for the little King." She lowered her voice, for Quendreda was now Queen and ruled with an iron hand. No one was allowed even to mention the name of King Kenelm.

"Yes," said the Archbishop quietly, and leaned close to listen.

"I have a cow," said the old lady. "My cow is pure white, very gentle and beautiful."

The Archbishop sighed and leaned back. It was clearly going to be a long story. The Archbishop's secretary coughed impatiently and made shuffling movements with his feet. Wilfred gestured to him to be patient. "Every day," continued the old lady, "she goes off into the wood, and though I've followed her, she doesn't eat anything. She just stands under a thorn tree all day, and when she comes home in the evening she looks plump and happy, and gives delicious milk."

She stopped and looked in a meaningful way at the Archbishop.

"I see," he said vaguely, since she had obviously reached the end of her story and was expecting some reaction.

"My lord," she said insistently, "don't you see?"

"Errm, no, not quite," he said apologetically. "Would you like me to bless your cow?"

She rolled her eyes to the skies. "My lord, call off your search of the whole forest. Just follow my cow, she'll take you to the little King. It's obvious as the ring on your finger that he must be buried by the thorn bush."

The Archbishop slapped his forehead. "Of course," he cried. "The verse the dove dropped –

> In Clent Cow-pasture under a thorn,
> Of head bereft lies Kenelm, King born."

And so it proved. The next day the men dug under the thorn tree where the cow always stood and found the little King's body. They placed it on a stretcher and started to carry it back to Winchcombe.

Another miracle occurred a few minutes later. Every time the men put down the stretcher to rest, a spring of crystal-clear water would gush forth. The men could take a drink and then, refreshed, carry on their journey.

As the procession entered Winchcombe, Quendreda stood at the palace window reading a prayer book backwards. As she saw the Archbishop and his men enter bearing the stretcher with her brother's body, her eyes sprang from her head and she ran screaming away and was never seen again.

Kenelm was buried near his father in the Abbey, and Winchcombe became a place of pilgrimage where people came from miles around to pray at the shrine of the spring saint.

Kenelm is said to have died in 821, having briefly succeeded his father King Kenulf (796–821). In the 16th century the Abbey was destroyed, leaving only a cross in the middle of a field to show where it once stood. In 1815 the site was excavated and two Saxon stone coffins were found. One contained the bones of a grown man (possibly King Kenulf), the other those of a child and beside the child's bones lay a long knife. The coffins were transferred to St Peter's Church, Winchcombe.

The last of the springs which marked the body's passage is called St Kenelm's Well on the Sudely estate on the hill above the town.

Sudeley Castle and gardens are open to the public. Winchcombe is just north-east of Cheltenham on the B4632.

HERTFORDSHIRE

THE WICKED LADY: MARKYATE

17TH CENTURY

When she was still only thirteen Lady Catherine Ferrers was married by her parents to an older man she scarcely knew. She had been alone with Sir Simon Fanshaw only once, when he came to ask for her hand in marriage, and although she had danced with him at a few parties, he was almost a total stranger to her. Still, she was not unhappy to be married. She would have pretty dresses, her own house in London, and be able to invite her friends and go out without her parents telling her what to do all the time.

Within a week, however, she began to have her doubts. Simon was dull and quiet, he hated going out and had only come up to London in order to find a suitable girl to marry. In fact, he intended to close up the town house and retire to the country. Nothing Catherine could say would change his mind. The best she could hope for was a two-week holiday in London each year.

In their country house of Markyate Cell, Catherine was soon desperately bored. She knew very few people in the neighbourhood, and those she met she considered old and stuffy. Exploring the attics one day in an attempt to pass the time, she discovered an old chest full of costumes, left over from some long-ago party. She began to try them on. The highwayman's suit fitted her perfectly. A few days before, pressing various carvings in her wood-panelled bedroom, she had discovered a hidden staircase, which gave her direct access to the grounds. An incredible idea began to form in her head.

Simon retired each night to his study to read and doze. He went to bed at around eleven, and they slept in separate bedrooms.

So one night, disguising herself in the highwayman's costume, she crept down the secret staircase, saddled her horse and rode quietly through the woods. A few miles away she came to the main road, Watling Street. There she held up her first coach.

Within months she had become the terror of the neighbourhood. The valuables she took – pearl and diamond necklaces and earrings from the ladies, watches and fobs from the gentlemen, and money from both – she hid in the back of her wardrobe, along with her disguise.

She became friendly with another highwayman, Ralph Chaplin, and together they wreaked havoc on passing traffic. Life had become fun again, but it was a dangerous game. One night, while Catherine was in bed with a cold, Ralph was shot on Finchley Common and never came home. Even this did not deter her. She was a little more cautious, but by now she could not give up the excitement of her secret night life.

But one night she too made a fatal error. She held up a coach near No Man's Land Common. She checked inside the carriage, but failed to spot a man asleep beneath his cloak. As she relieved the driver of his purse, the passenger leaned out and shot her. In pain and bleeding profusely, she just managed to stay on her horse, and struggled home. She crawled up the stairs and into her bed, but she was too weak from loss of blood to call out for help.

X X X

The next morning the maid knocked at the door in vain. In the end she called her master, and the horrified Sir Simon broke down the door and discovered his beautiful, wild young wife, still dressed in her highwayman's costume, lying dead from gun-shot wounds. He buried her quietly and hoped that was the last he would hear of her.

No such luck. Catherine's ghost started to appear in the kitchen and on the great staircase, yawning and languid (for she was usually tired in the morning after riding around during the hours of darkness). At night she would be seen, report had it, galloping hell-for-leather through the surrounding forests. Simon Fanshaw closed up the house and decided to move to London after all. Catherine would have been pleased, but her ghost was left behind in Markyate.

In 1840 there was a serious fire in the house, and when the workmen came to fix the damage she terrified them by swinging from the branch of a nearby sycamore tree in broad daylight. The workmen fled and the owner had difficulty finding anyone to finish the job. Once she dropped down from the tree into the middle of a parish tea, terrifying the vicar and the village ladies. But she got most enjoyment from riding at night along the lanes she had known. She can still be seen on her coal-black horse galloping wildly along the streets around Markyate, her eyes shining with excitement through her highwayman's mask.

Markyate Cell was rebuilt in 1840 on the site of the Tudor house. No Man's Land Common, near Weathampstead off the A1(M) on the B651, where Catherine was shot, is now a recreation area, and a local child-friendly pub has been renamed The Wicked Lady. *A plaque in the pub commemorates her story.*

KENT

THE DEVIL DROPS A TOWN: CANTERBURY AND WHITSTABLE

After the death of Saint Thomas à Becket (see pages 32–38), the town of Canterbury grew larger and richer as people flocked to pray at the new shrine in the Cathedral. Unfortunately, the richer the town grew, the greedier and more selfish its citizens became, and after a few hundred years the Devil saw his opportunity. His interest aroused, he flew around the town and saw that soon he could claim the inhabitants' souls for himself. But he knew that as long as the monks prayed at the shrine of Saint Thomas he could never gain power. Only if they stopped would he have a chance. And one day his chance came.

It was an important festival. There were three times more

pilgrims in Canterbury than had ever visited before and the monks were exhausted with praying and organizing and feeding the guests. At last the monks who had prayed all day went to bed, but Brother James, who should have rung the bell for the change of shift, fell asleep again before he had done his duty. So no one rang and the night shift brothers stayed in their beds. The shrine was left unattended, and the Devil saw his chance. His moment had come.

He swooped down on the town like a huge bat, and picked up as much of the town as he could in one go. He flew off with the armful of buildings and flung them in the sea. Then he sped back for more.

Asleep in his cell, Brother Michael tossed and turned. He was thirsty, he had a dry throat and the smell of sulphur filled his cell. Suddenly his eyes snapped open. "What a strange smell," he thought. As he lay quietly on his hard bed, wondering whether he should get up and pour himself a drink, he heard a strange swishing sound, as though a large bird were flying past. Curious and a little frightened, he slipped from his bed, fumbled to put on his cassock and crept out of his cell into the cloisters. Looking up into the sky where the moon shone brightly, he could just see in the distance an eerie shape flying away towards the coast.

Around him all was silent, and suddenly Brother Michael realized what was missing – the soft sound of his fellow monks praying quietly around the shrine of Saint Thomas. Brother Michael picked up his skirts and ran swiftly, despite his age, into the Cathedral. It was true, it was empty.

Suddenly in the sky above, the mysterious dark figure returned. Brother Michael hid behind a column and watched in disbelief. The Devil flew quietly past the Cathedral to the outskirts of town. There he scooped up as many shops and houses as he could carry and then flew slowly back over the Cathedral, his wings beating heavily with the weight of his load. Straining his eyes and ears, Brother Michael heard a splash in the distance as the Devil disposed of his burden in the sea and returned.

The monk waited no longer. He ran as fast as he could to the bell tower, seized hold of the nearest rope and began to pull the great bell, known as Harry, as loudly as he could.

The Devil was just flying along with his next load and had reached the coast, but he got such a shock of disappointment at hearing the Cathedral bell tolling that he dropped the houses he was carrying, not in the sea, but on a nearby hillside.

By the time Brother Michael's fellow monks had emerged from their cells, rubbing sleepy eyes and looking around in alarm, the danger had passed and the Devil had disappeared. But Canterbury had lost part of its inhabitants and buildings, dropped into the sea, while the last armful lay scattered on a coastal hillside. These people were astonished to find their houses transported several miles from their original positions, dumped any which way, just as they had been dropped by the startled Devil. They decided – since they really had no choice – to leave their houses there, and start a new town on that higgledy-piggledy hillside. The new town was to be known as Whitstable.

Whitstable is eight miles away from Canterbury. If you go to either place, see if you can spot any unusual or unexpected gaps in the houses.

Bell Harry Tower can still be seen at Canterbury Cathedral and it contains the oldest of cathedral bells still in use. Bell Harry was given to the Cathedral by Prior Henry of . Eastry in the fourteenth century. The bell was re-cast in 1635 and weighs 900 kilograms.

KENT

POCAHONTAS: GRAVESEND

1617

Pocahontas had been to London and met the King and Queen! She had stood amazed, looking at the city, with its stone houses and the thousands of people who lived there, so different from the forests of Virginia in America where she had been born, or even from the tiny wooden settlement of

Jamestown where the English traders were trying to build a European-style town in America.

She was staying at The Bell, an inn just off busy, noisy Fleet Street, and the noise of the traffic and street calls was terrific. And the people were so smelly. Back home she and all her family and friends had bathed every day in the river, but good heavens, these Europeans took at most one bath a year! The stench was revolting.

She was now used to the clothes, the dress with its long skirts that made running almost impossible, the lace collar that itched, the funny little hat that got in the way at first. But she had never worn them for so long. Back in America, she had worn European dress for a smart dinner, or for church, but never day in, day out for months at a time.

Still, she had her husband, John Rolfe, with her, and her little son Thomas. And the other day she had even met Captain John Smith, the man she had saved from a horrible death years ago back in America. Captain Smith had been captured by Pocahontas' father, Powhatan, back in 1607 when Pocahontas was only about twelve years old, and sentenced to have his brains smashed out with stone tomahawks. Captain Smith was one of the leaders of the English settlers at Jamestown, a rough and tough adventurer, while Powhatan was the most important chief of the Algonkian Indian tribes.

Pocahontas had been horrified at the sight of the preparations to kill Captain Smith. The Englishman had smiled kindly at her even as he lay bound and waiting for judgement, and she had felt sorry for him. As the executioners raised their tomahawks in the air to kill him, the little Indian girl ran forwards and laid her cheek on his.

"Spare him, father," she had begged. Powhatan was not convinced, but his daughter pleaded so earnestly that he had finally agreed. The next day Captain Smith was escorted back to the settlement and after a few months left to return to England.

Pocahontas had been sad at his departure. She had begun to visit Jamestown occasionally, curious at the way of life of these strange people who had come to live on their shores and who had such different customs. She had become friendly with John Rolfe, a businessman who had come out to grow tobacco, and when he asked her to be his wife she had agreed happily. John was kind and handsome, and he told her he loved her.

"Come with me to England," he asked, and she had jumped at the chance. She had taken an English name, Rebecca, and been baptized a Christian, but at heart she remained a native American. The life in London had been thrilling, especially meeting the King and Queen, but now she felt ill and longed to return home.

John Rolfe looked worriedly at his wife. She would not even be well enough to visit the Court and see the Queen again that afternoon. He sat down and wrote a note of apology, and Queen Anne was so worried about her American visitor, that she sent her own doctor. But it was all to no avail. Pocahontas, far from her native country and forests, became sicker and sicker, and John Rolfe decided the only solution was to return to America with her as quickly as possible. They booked a passage on the *George*, and set off down the Thames to the port of Gravesend, where the ship was to take on its final fresh food and water before the long trip across the ocean.

But there Rebecca, who had been called Pocahontas, became too ill even to sail home. She was brought ashore, and died in John's arms.

She was buried in the Church of St George's at Gravesend, and a little statue stands there today, with her back to the shopping centre, a feather flying in her hair, a fur over her shoulder, the first native American girl to cross the sea.

X X X

St George's Church burnt down in 1727, though it was rebuilt in 1731. The church register states: "1617, March 21st. Rebecca Wrolf, Wyffe of Thomas [sic] Wrolf Gent, a Virginian Lady borne, was buried in the channcell."

The Bell Inn where the Rolfes stayed is now the Café Rouge, Ludgate Hill off Fleet Street, London.

LONDON

BURTON'S TENT: MORTLAKE

1890

Richard Francis Burton was sitting in his tent reading when he heard the men attacking. He dropped his book, *The Arabian Nights* (which he had been reading with difficulty since it was written in Arabic), and picked up his gun, which always lay ready loaded by his bed. Outside he could hear shouting and the sound of fighting. Peering cautiously around the entrance to the tent as he took aim at the intruders, he could just see the tents of his companions also under attack.

After an hour of fighting Richard and two of his friends managed to escape to a boat moored behind them on the river bank, but it had been a terrible fight. Richard had been injured by a spear in the cheek, Lieutenant John Hanning Speke had been hit very hard by a war club on the chest, and one friend had been killed on the way to the boat. The expedition, which should have gone to the interior of Africa, was abandoned.

X X X

Richard Burton was born in 1821. When he left school he joined the army, though he was not really interested in being a soldier. He wanted to be an adventurer. It was 1842, and Britain ruled over India, so he was sent out to join a regiment near Bombay. There was nothing much to do so Richard began to collect monkeys and soon had about 40 different types which he taught to sit at table. His servants had to serve them tea, while he tried to make conversation with them and understand their language. He tried to write a dictionary of monkey-language, and managed to work out sixty words.

In his free time he would put on a disguise. Colouring his skin brown with henna, and hiding behind a long beard, he would pretend to be called Mirza Abdullah, and would go round the streets of Bombay selling trays of sweets and dates, and drinking coffee and playing chess. His disguise was very successful and no one ever recognized him, so he decided to try a dangerous challenge.

Mecca is the most holy town of the Moslems, and non-Moslems may not go there. If they are discovered, they risk death. But Richard's disguise and his acting were so convincing that during the whole trip to Mecca no one suspected him. He even managed to get right up to the Ka'aba, the sacred shrine towards which all Moslems turn when praying, wherever they are in the world.

X X X

After this adventure, Richard decided to try and find the source of the River Nile. No one knew where the Nile started, although it clearly came from somewhere in the middle of Africa, before reaching the sea in Egypt. The first expedition ended in the disaster described at the beginning of the story, but Richard and his friend, John Hanning Speke, would not give up.

They returned to Africa two years later. This time they prepared masses of provisions for the journey: bags of beads to give the local people as presents, salt, pepper, 20 pounds of sugar, five boxes of tea, a box of cigars, 60 bottles of brandy. They took quantities of weapons in case they were attacked, including several huge boxes of gunpowder. They even carried with them some camp furniture – two tents (one small and one large), a table, two chairs. There were also boxes of navigational instruments, such as chronometers and compasses, and lots of paper, pads, diaries and pens. In case of problems, they took with them a toolbox with 70 pounds of nails, four umbrellas, 2,000 fish hooks, and of course a Union Jack flag. They then needed to find 50 men and donkeys to help them carry their luggage. Richard Burton and John Hanning Speke did not believe in travelling light.

But the expedition was again unlucky and badly organized. The men forgot to unload the donkeys when they went through a stream with the sugar, tea, and salt, so it all dissolved and floated away. Only the cigars were left, and they became soggy.

Then the box carrying the scientific instruments was not strapped on properly, and fell off, breaking all the compasses.

When they crossed a waterfall, John lost his spare boots and the table and chair disappeared. Richard became very upset at the loss of the furniture and sent out a search party. He felt he could not possibly carry on with nowhere to sit and write.

Then a swarm of bees attacked the men, and the porter carrying all the writing material threw the box down a cliff while trying to escape from the bees, so Richard had no paper to write on anyway!

Both Englishmen became very sick and the porters had to help them up onto their donkeys each morning since they were too weak to walk. At last they came to a steep and stony hill covered in thorn trees. Half way up, John's donkey fell over dead from tiredness, but they still continued to struggle up the hill. At the top they looked out and saw a big sheet of water, Lake Tanganyika, the longest lake in the world, 400 miles long.

A few days later, and after nearly eight months of trekking, Richard and John entered a little town called Ujiji, where a few years later more famous explorers called Stanley and Livingstone were to meet. They stayed and rested for a while, and wondered whether this was the source of the Nile.

Soon John felt a little better, and he set off for a bit of extra exploring while Richard stayed behind, writing up his diary and resting. The two men were happy to have a few days' peace from one another, since they had begun to argue. Unfortunately for Richard, John alone discovered another huge lake nearby, which he called Lake Victoria, and which he was sure was the source of the Nile. It turned out to be so.

Poor Richard returned to England, only to find that John Hanning Speke had become famous, while no one even knew that it had been his expedition.

X X X

As he grew older, Richard Burton, helped by his wife Isabel, started to translate some of the stories he had come across in his travels. The most famous of these is *The Arabian Nights*, or *The 1,001 Nights*. King Shahriyar, who had been betrayed by his first wife, vowed that every day he would marry a girl and then behead her the next morning. This went on for some time, and many girls perished. Then it was the turn of the beautiful Scheherazade, daughter of the Grand Vizier, but she had a clever plan. Each night she told the King a wonderful story, but she never finished the story before morning, and always left the end of the tale for the following night. So the King could never execute her or he would never know what happened to Sinbad, Aladdin, Haroun al Rashid, Ali Baba or many other now-famous heroes. These were the stories which Richard Burton translated.

When he died, his wife prepared a magnificent tomb for him. She brought his body back from his travels, and ordered the building of a large Arab tent, 18 feet high, made of stone and white Italian marble with a nine-pointed star on top. In it she put some of the favourite things he had always carried with him on his travels – a special lamp, a water pipe, some pictures and some books. Perhaps she put a copy of the Arabian Nights there.

Sir Richard Burton is buried at the Catholic Church of St Mary Magdalen at Barnes in south-west London. The shape of a full-size Bedouin tent, it nestles incongruously among the crosses and angels in a typical English churchyard. His coffin is laid on one side of the tent, and his wife's on the other.

Because of vandals, the entrance to the tent was sealed up, but you can climb up a ladder at the back, and look down through a hole in the roof.

LONDON

THE TOWER BEAR

1235

Ben and Talia had run away from their nanny, Mary. She had only looked the other way for ten seconds and – they were gone. Mary had searched and searched all over the Tower, from the lowest dungeons to the highest turrets of the battlements. Eventually she had been forced to report them missing to the

Lost Property Office and had gone home to break the news to their mother.

Meanwhile Ben and Talia were enjoying their new-found freedom. They had given Mary the slip by hiding behind a curtain, and then they had run giggling round the corner. It was as easy as that. Talia had always been good at running away, but Ben was a mere beginner and could not run very fast, so he was particularly pleased to have been so successful in one of his earliest full-scale attempts.

The fun continued as closing time approached. The Beefeaters who guard the Tower, dressed in smart scarlet, carried out their last patrols, failed to spot the children, and locked up the great gates.

As silence fell, Ben and Talia looked at one another uneasily. Suddenly hiding did not seem such a good idea. Ben began to whimper. He was hungry, he wanted his supper, he wanted his parents, he wanted his teddy, and he even wanted his bed. Talia too was not happy.

Night fell and the children huddled together, seeking warmth and comfort by keeping close under Talia's jacket. It was cold, dark and very frightening. Talia had discovered a couple of fluff-covered crisps in her pocket and they had shared them. It was not much of a supper. Talia thought about all the prisoners who had been locked in the Tower and had never left it. Ben thought about his teddy and his mummy.

Suddenly a dark shadow loomed. It rose and rose from the other side of the large gloomy room. Larger and larger, a menacing black shape that looked very like a bear.

The children were so frightened they could not even scream. Mouths wide open, eyes huge in terror, they could only stare in anguished silence.

The bear – it was a bear! – growled, and began to come closer, step by step.

"No, no," Talia gasped, but Ben just gulped. The bear was only a foot away and still coming ever closer. It was on them! The children closed their eyes and waited for the end.

x x x

The bear, a large adult polar bear, lumbered easily through the room. Being only a ghost of a bear, he did not pay any attention to the children huddled by the wall. He was on his way down to the river to fish for his daily food, ghostly Thames fish. Around his neck, had their eyes been open, the children could have just made out a collar and a strong rope preventing his escape from the Tower.

The bear had arrived at the Tower over 700 years previously and his diet had at first caused such problems to his keeper that in desperation he had asked the sheriff of London for help. The sheriff came with his colleagues to inspect the situation.

On their arrival at the Tower they had first been shown the three leopards, a splendid gift a few years earlier from the Emperor of the Holy Roman Empire, Frederick II, to King Henry III of England. On their arrival in 1235 the keeper had lodged them in what became known as the Lion Tower, a small-ish building which was only used for storing old bits and pieces that nobody needed. The sheriff and his men gazed in awe at the sleek coats and powerful paws and jaws of the big cats.

Then the keeper showed them a truly amazing animal. It was a huge, strange beast with a long tail between its eyes and flapping ears that drew crowds of Londoners who had never seen such a bizarre animal. Known as an elephant, it had come from Africa, a gift from the King of France who had heard of the success of the Emperor's gift of leopards. The town officials gasped in wonderment, and held on to their hats as the elephant's front tail came out towards them curiously like an exploring hand. They backed away in awe.

The keeper explained to the officials that while the elephant ate hay and grass which the king was happy to supply from the regular stable supplies, and the leopards ate meat which his huntsmen could supply, the quantities of fish which the polar bear needed were huge and there was no money available. The keeper himself could not spend the necessary time fishing and he was at his wits' end.

The sheriff, much taken with all the animals, and with the white bear in particular, conferred with his colleagues. It was soon decided that the city of London would take responsibility for the bear. They offered four pence a day which was enough to buy food and even leave a bit extra for the keeper. In a moment of extreme generosity and reasonable concern for the safety of the citizens of the town, they also agreed to provide a collar and a long strong rope so that the bear could go down to the river and fish for himself on the banks. Soon the polar bear became a familiar sight on the muddy banks of the Thames.

X X X

The ghostly bear walked through the two little children huddled in the corner. His rope trailed behind him. He walked through the wall, down the corridor to the river. He fished contentedly in the muddy water until he caught his ghostly fish, and then he returned happily to the Lion Tower. Ben and Talia clung to one another in amazement. Then, through the darkness of the night, they heard the sound of huge keys turning and bolts being scraped back.

"Children, there you are," cried their mother and she scooped Ben and Talia into her arms and kissed them in relief. Then she slapped them soundly, because she was so relieved. They did not mind, they were so happy to be found.

"Mummy," said Talia when she had caught her breath after their father had also kissed and then smacked them. "We nearly got eaten by a bear."

"Yes, dear," said their mother. "Now let's go home and have some supper."

Nobody saw the Beefeaters, who had opened the gates to the distraught parents, exchanging glances. They knew all about the ghostly Tower bear.

The Lion Tower stood just outside the Middle Tower, on the present site of the public entrance, where you buy your tickets and souvenirs. In 1834 the Royal animal collection had out-grown the Tower and was moved to Regents Park where it became the current London Zoo.

LONDON

THE SEEDSEEKER: KEW GARDENS

1824

On the banks of the lake in Kew Gardens stands a tall slim fir tree, a Douglas Fir. Many years ago a young man set out for the land of America to collect the seeds of the many different plants and trees unknown in England. Among the many varieties

he sent back was the Douglas Fir, now one of the most important trees used for building work.

x x x

David Douglas was born in 1799 in a humble cottage in Scone
in Scotland, where his father was a stonemason, making grave-
stones in the local churchyard. As David grew up he knew he
definitely did not want to do what his father did. He was more
interested in birds and plants, and very soon he was apprenticed
as a gardener in the grounds of the local Earl's house.

There he learned all he could about seeds and cuttings, and
when a famous professor, Dr Hooker, wanted a guide and helper
for a trip to the Scottish Islands, David got the job. Later
Dr Hooker was to become Director of Kew Gardens, already
well-known for its thousands of different kinds of fruit trees,
roses and shrubs.

Dr Hooker was an important figure in the world of plants, and
when, in 1823, the Horticultural Society asked his advice about
who they should send out to America to collect many different
sorts of new seeds and samples of unknown trees, he immediately recommended his young guide from Scotland. He was young,
fit, enthusiastic, and knew all about existing plants, said
Dr Hooker.

When David received the letter, he could hardly speak with
excitement. "Father, mother," he shouted, rushing into
the room where they sat quietly reading and sewing. "I'm to
go to America! I'm to sail in a week!" and he danced with
excitement.

His parents were less happy. America was very far away – nearly
two months by ship – and could be dangerous. Apart from the
voyage there, the centre of the continent was almost unknown,
just forests, rivers and mountains, and the local inhabitants were
fierce and uncivilized.

But David brushed aside their concerns. "It's the chance of a lifetime," he said, and they softened when they saw how excited he was. He left the next morning by stagecoach and soon he was aboard the *Ann Maria* which was to take him on his first voyage abroad.

X X X

As soon as he arrived in New York he started to collect seeds. Then he travelled on by steamship, stagecoach and canal-boat, seeking out new varieties.

One day he had an unpleasant adventure. He had found an interesting kind of oak tree and wished to climb up and pick some acorns. Since it was hot, he took off his coat and left it with his guide, a runaway Virginian slave, but no sooner had David climbed high into the tree, than the man grabbed his coat and ran away with it. David slithered down as fast as he could, but by the time he got down, the man was far away. In his coat he had lost all his notes on the seeds he had found so far, and quite a lot of money. But there was nothing to be done. He stamped his foot in anger, then shrugged his shoulders and climbed back up the tree to get the acorns. These he tied in his neck-cloth and went back to the carriage he had borrowed.

"Come on, giddup," he called to the horse, and shook the reins encouragingly. But the beast would not move. After several minutes of trying, he got down and went round to the horse's head. The beast looked obstinately at him, and David ended up dragging him down the path back home. When they finally reached the stables several hours later, the owner explained that the horse only understood French, having belonged to a French family.

David ran his hands through his hair in despair. What a day! He had lost his money, his seeds and his coat, and then been lumbered with a French-speaking horse...

X X X

In spite of this setback, David Douglas collected many plant samples and seeds, and returned to London in early 1824, having been extremely seasick during the whole voyage, but with all his seeds in good condition. The Horticultural Society received them eagerly and immediately set their gardeners to work growing them.

They were so pleased with his efforts that they decided to send him off again within a few months. This time he was to go to the American Columbia River, where the city of Portland, Oregon now stands on the North West Pacific coast. His ship, the *William and Mary*, survived a huge storm and came in to land. As the ship rounded the point, David caught his first sight of what was to be called the Douglas Fir. The tree stood straight and slender, with deep yellow-green leaves and spreading branches. While the upper ones curved to the sky, the lower branches drooped to the ground. David stood at the ship's rail and vowed to collect some cones and seeds from that tree.

When the ship had docked, he unloaded his equipment. There were only a few houses here, and he rigged a tent for the first few weeks. Later he built himself a hut from deerskin and when this became too cold, a little house of bark.

Every day he was out in the forest or travelling up the river in his canoe, picking berries and seeds, and taking cuttings. He found many new plants this way, plants which are now common in our gardens in Britain.

But he still had a problem with his beautiful fir tree. The one he had seen from the ship, like the others he found later, was too big. It was over 70 metres high, and 16 metres round the trunk at waist level. It was too big to chop down with his little hatchet. Normally he would shoot cones down with his musket, but these firs were too tall and the cones were out of reach of his buckshot. After the last episode, where he lost his money and his notes, he was uneasy about climbing such large trees, and anyway the trunk was too smooth and the cones very high up. He began to dream at night about his cones, always hanging just out of reach.

x x x

When the *William and Mary* set off back home, he sent his collection, carefully packed, back to England. It took him two weeks just to pack it, and by the time he had finished there were 24 large bundles, a huge seed chest and a box of birds and animals.

David himself decided to stay on for an extra year and try to cross the whole continent of America overland. Above all, he felt he could not leave without his fir seeds. After the ship had left, as he sat sorting through his things, a small Native American boy, the son of Chumtalia, a local chief, slid into his room.

"I have heard you want cones," the boy said without hesitation. David Douglas blinked. He had not been able to bring himself to start packing, for he could not bear to leave the area without the seeds of that glorious fir tree.

"Yes," he agreed, looking curiously at the boy. He was about eleven years old, thin and wiry, but with muscular arms and an intelligent look. His English was perfect.

"I'm a very good climber," said the boy, and it was not a boast, just a statement. "My father said you want some cones from the trees on the point." He lifted one eyebrow slightly, because he thought the Scotsman slightly mad, and he did not see why anyone would want such a strange thing. Still, he had been there for months and they had got used to him and even a little fond of him.

"Come with me," he said. David stumbled to his feet, grabbed his hat and collecting bag and abandoned his packing in delight.

An hour later he held in his palm the first cone which the boy had thrown down for him. He was so happy two little tears of joy trickled from his eyes. When the boy came down David hugged him and thanked him. Chumtalia's son disentangled himself, bowed gravely and melted back into the forest.

X X X

Now David could concentrate on his packing. He took crates full of paper to wrap the seeds he would find, but only two shirts, two handkerchiefs, a blanket, a cloak and one pair of shoes for himself. He did not even take any stockings or socks! He set off up the Columbia River for the Spokane River, climbing the Blue Mountains on the way.

One day some Native Americans brought him several large seeds, seeds which they usually carried in their pouches to chew on when they were hungry. They told him the seeds came from a big pine tree called the sugar pine, with fat cones over a foot long, and he received them gratefully. Now he had a new obsession. He had to find the tree itself and obtain some fresh seeds. To have a good chance of growing back in England, the seeds needed to be collected fresh.

As he travelled he kept a look out for the sugar pine, but he never saw it. After six months, although he had found many other plants, including his fir, the sugar pine still eluded him. He was in rags, with sore eyes, tired and hungry, when he heard a rumour about some of these trees. He immediately set off, and there they were – huge trees with straight trunks and no branches, and right at the top, the huge fat cones.

David rubbed his eyes, which were red and painful through infection and tiredness, and then took careful aim. The cones were so big he thought he could probably manage to hit them. As the shots rang out through the forest, some Native Americans hunting nearby heard the noise. They looked at one another and then without further ado, picked up their spears and crept towards the source of the noise. As David was gleefully scooping up his sugar cones, eight large and hostile Native Americans stepped from behind the trees and stood silently watching him, holding their weapons threateningly.

They were painted with red earth and heavily armed with bows and arrows, as well as their spears of bone. Sharp flint knives hung at their waist, and their expressions were not friendly. David clutched the cones to his chest, determined not to lose the seeds for which he had been searching for so long. He quietly fumbled for his tobacco pouch and offered the Native Americans the contents. Then as they accepted the whole pouch, he backed off, never taking his eyes off them, and returned shaking to his camp.

The next morning three grizzly bears attacked the camp and David decided to move on. The place was unlucky. But his bad luck was not over. Crossing the Santiam River the luggage spilled into the water, and weeks of collecting was lost. Only the precious sugar pine and the Douglas fir cones were saved because David was carrying them on his own back.

It was time to return home. Travelling slowly and making up the lost collection as best he could, David arrived at Fort Garry (now Winnipeg). From there he could catch a boat and return to England where he was welcomed as a hero by the Horticultural Society.

Kew Gardens is in south-west London.

A Douglas fir, Pseudotsuga menziesii, *stands on the western bank of the long lake in Kew Gardens, opposite the largest island. These pines have transformed forestry schemes throughout the British Isles and become one of the world's most important woods for building. The sugar pine at Kew Gardens,* Pinus lambertiana, *is planted between the lake and the Thames and is one of the closest to the river, on a little hillock by a small white hut. Both trees are descendants from Douglas's cones.*

Among the now common garden plants David Douglas

*brought back are penstemons, wild hyacinths, flowering currants, Oregon grapes, several types of honeysuckle, some lupins, poached egg plant (*limnanthes douglasii*), gaillardias and several new rhododendrons, as well as numerous other pines.*

David Douglas finally perished on one of his trips. In 1834, aged only 35, he visited Hawaii to explore the volcanoes there. Although he had been warned about a series of bulltraps, large pits concealed with branches and grass to catch wild bulls, he stepped too close to one of them and slipped in. He was gored to death by the bull trapped there.

LONDON

HEIL HITLER:
CARLTON HOUSE TERRACE

1934

"Heil Hitler!" shouted the doorman, and the ambassador quietly replied, "Heil Hitler."

"Grrrr." Under his breath Giro, the ambassador's large Alsatian dog, growled. He knew his master did not like the greeting, which was always accompanied by a straight raised right arm, and often a click together of the heels.

When people had started saluting a couple of years before, Giro had started barking loudly and pretending to attack, and at first his master, Ambassador Leopold von Hoesch, had laughed. But after a while he had told Giro to stop it.

Now Giro no longer barked, but he growled quietly and once recently, when a pair of shiny brown boots were very close to his nose and the owner had cried, "Heil Hitler!" with particular vigour, Giro had not been able to resist. He had sunk his teeth into a gleaming leather calf just as the owner clicked his heels. Ambassador von Hoesch was astonished. Giro had been his companion for many years and he had always been well-behaved and friendly. The ambassador had pulled Giro off and apologized to the man, a messenger from Berlin, but Giro could feel that his master was not really displeased with him.

The problem was that von Hoesch really sympathized with the dog's dislike of Nazis. Since Adolf Hitler had taken power in Germany the year before, his job had proved almost impossible. In his elegant study at 9 Carlton House Terrace, Ambassador Leopold von Hoesch read through the new laws and policies of Nazi Germany in increasing despair. How could he represent a country which believed in such things? A country in which Jews and gypsies were not considered real people, which was arming for war against the rest of Europe? Whenever he went to official parties in London, people began to avoid him, and both he and his country were regarded with suspicion.

x x x

When Giro died, at a ripe old age, he was buried in the embassy garden with a small gravestone. Two years later, worn out with the stress and worry of his job, von Hoesch himself followed his dog.

His successor, Joachim von Ribbentrop, was a very different

man. When he was introduced to the King he raised his hand and shouted "Heil Hitler" with great enthusiasm. He ripped out the old study, threw out all the previous Ambassador's paintings, and would have knocked down the whole building had it not been protected by English law. Luckily he never noticed the little gravestone outside, under the tree next to the embassy. "Giro, a true companion. February 1934."

The gravestone is under the tree, to the left of the steps, next to 9 Carlton House Terrace in the centre of London. You can see it easily through the railing from the pavement if you know where to look.

Ribbentrop left the Embassy in March 1938 and war between Britain and Germany was declared in 1939. Five doors down at number 4, General de Gaulle set up the Headquarters of the Free French, the French anti-Nazi government. After the war, the German embassy moved to Belgrave Square.

LONDON

GANESH: NEASDEN

1996

Parvati sat in her luxurious palace and looked out glumly over the surrounding mountains. She was bored, fed up and lonely. Her husband, Shiva, was always away at work and even when he was home he never had time for her. Whenever she complained he just said he had a lot of praying to do, and he also told her he had to keep dancing on top of the world to keep it going.

Needless to say, Parvati was not impressed. She was a beautiful woman and whenever Shiva was home she made a special effort, wearing her best clothes and brushing her hair until it shone, but all to no avail.

Shiva was handsome in an interesting way. He had a blue throat where he had gulped down some poison spat out by the wicked cobra Vasuki. He dared not swallow it in case it killed him, but he had saved the world from the poison even though it had done strange things to his neck. He also had a third eye in the centre of his forehead, to keep some light for the world when his other two eyes were closed.

Nevertheless Parvati loved him. But one day, when he had been away for several weeks, she went down to the river for a swim in a sad and mournful mood. "If only I had children," she said. "At least I'd have someone to play with."

As she sat drying off on the river bank she glumly squeezed some earth between her fingers. It was like clay and stuck together. As she sat sadly moulding shapes with her hands, she thought the little lump of clay began to look like a baby. She rolled a fat little ball and poked a belly button in its middle. She pinched out some arms and legs and began to feel quite pleased with her work. She took a little twig and drew some eyes, and a mouth under a little round button of a nose.

"I wish he was real," she sighed. "He looks sweet, with his little fat tummy."

Suddenly a thought occurred to her. She was, after all, a goddess, married to one of the most powerful of gods. That must be worth something. She breathed on the clay, the way she had heard that gods and goddesses could breathe life into things.

The little lump of clay opened its eyes and blinked. It had worked!

As she sat in awe and happiness admiring her new baby, he opened his mouth and yawned. Soon he began to cry. Parvati realized he was a real baby and was probably hungry. She picked him up and carried him home, her heart leaping with joy.

X X X

Parvati called her little boy Ganesh, and he grew strong and jolly. He was always laughing and chuckling and she loved him dearly. They were always together, especially since this time Shiva was away for several years.

One day Parvati went down to the river to swim again, as she often did. Ganesh always came too, not to swim for he did not like to get his face wet, but to sit on the bank and make mud pies and clay sandcastles.

Suddenly Shiva appeared. He saw his beautiful wife swimming in the river, and he saw a little boy that was not his playing on the bank. The child saw a strange man with a snake round his bluish neck and a trident in his hand approaching his mother. He screamed to warn her and ran to kick the stranger. Shiva was overcome with anger and pulled out his sword. With one fell swoop he chopped Ganesh's head off.

From the middle of the river, Parvati saw her child lying fatally injured and shouted to her husband, "What have you done? You've killed my baby. Do something, do something!"

Tears were streaming down her face. Shiva was horrified at his deed. Without a word he ran back into the forest and looked for the first living thing he could find.

Within minutes he was back, carrying a replacement head. He stuck it on the little boy's shoulders and Ganesh sat up rubbing his head, as though he had done nothing worse than just bang it on a chair. Parvati was delighted. She threw her arms round first Ganesh, then Shiva. The family was happy again.

No one seemed to worry that the new head had once belonged to an elephant, and Ganesh was happy with his long useful new nose and big flapping new ears.

Ganesh can be found at the Shri Swaminarayan Mandir temple, 115–119 Brentfield Road, Neasden, NW10 8JP (off the North Circular Road), telephone: 0181 965 2651. His shrine is the first on the left as you enter. He has an elephant head, and rides on a mouse so that he can slip through holes or his steed can gnaw his way through obstructions. The mouse is carrying something sweet for him to eat. He likes his food, so is often brought edible presents. Above you can see his parents, Shiva and Parvati, with Shiva wearing Vasuki the serpent round his neck. There is also a column of stone carvings of Ganesh.

The temple took 27 months to build and is intended to last for a thousand years. The stone, brought from the quarries of Bulgaria and Italy, was shipped to India to carve, and then on to England. No steel or iron was used in the construction of the temple; all the pieces and slabs were carefully designed to slot together like a huge puzzle.

NORTHAMPTONSHIRE

THE TUNNELLING FIDDLER: TRIANGULAR LODGE

18TH CENTURY

In the late eighteenth century Lord Robert Cullen, owner of the Triangular Lodge, discovered the opening to an underground passage when searching for a missing dog one day. The tunnel was dank and dark, and looked very unsafe. An evil smell came from the opening. Lord Robert was unwilling to enter himself, being afraid of enclosed places, but he was very curious to know where the tunnel might lead.

"Fifty pounds to anyone who will follow it to the end," he

cried out. No one took up his offer, for the entrance looked very ominous.

Later that evening, the event was discussed in the local tavern. Harry Perkins, the fiddler engaged to entertain the drinkers that evening, was intrigued. His father had been a miner, and he was used to the idea of dark underground places. Besides, he could really do with fifty pounds. That would stop his wife Anne from nagging him all the time.

The next day he went up to the hall and asked for Lord Robert. Cullen was delighted with his offer, and immediately gave him the promised money, along with a supply of candles to light his way. Then the whole household accompanied Harry to the entrance to the tunnel.

He solemnly gave the money over to his wife's safekeeping, stuck a candle in his hat band, picked up his fiddle and set off. Just before he disappeared into the gloom, he turned and winked at his wife.

The music began to fade as he got further away. For a while they could just make out the strains of "Moll in the Wad", his favourite song, and then they could hear it no more. There was a deathly silence. The anxious bystanders waited an hour or more. Then as Anne began to grow tearful, two of Harry's friends reluctantly offered to go down in and try and find him.

When they returned, pale and dishevelled, they reported grim tidings. They had found a candle and a hat – and a bottomless pit. Anne began to wail in earnest, and was only eventually consoled by another hundred pounds from the guilt-stricken Lord Robert.

Two years later, Anne made her way up to the hall again. She had a letter she wanted to show Lord Robert. She was immediately shown in. The letter was from her husband, Harry. He told how he had fallen a long way down a hole, then had scrambled along more tunnels, fallen once again, and so continued, until eventually, he had fallen all the way to Australia, then newly discovered. He was now writing to his ever-loving wife, Anne, to ask her to join him.

Anne watched in silence as Lord Robert read the letter. She could see from his expression that he was impressed with the tale. Now was the moment to strike.

"The problem is, my lord," she began, "it's a long way to Australia, and I daren't take the same route my Harry took."

"No, quite, quite," said Lord Robert, scratching his wig.

"Given it was your Lordship sent my Harry down the hole," she continued, "do you think you could do the decent thing and provide me with the fare to join him, by ship, the regular way?"

"Yes, yes, of course, only thing to be done," agreed Lord Robert, and Anne Perkins left the hall clutching her travel money. Before anyone could change Cullen's mind, she had left the village to join Harry in Norwich, where he had been living since finding a secret way out of the tunnel.

Lord Robert Cullen had the entrance to the tunnel bricked up.

No one knows where the tunnel's entrance is any more. Sir Francis Tresham, one of the Guy Fawkes' plot conspirators, was the original owner and architect of the Triangular Lodge. Perhaps Sir Francis knew that his was to be a life of intrigue and that tunnels might come in handy. However, rather than Norwich or Australia, he ended up in the Tower where he died in great pain, possibly of poison. He was nevertheless tried and beheaded after his death.

The Lodge is open to the public and is in the grounds of Rushton Hall in Northamptonshire, just off the A6 near Desborough.

NORTHUMBERLAND

MY SISTER THE WORM: BAMBURGH AND SPINDLESTONE HEUGH

AD 550

King Ida of Northumbria was a great warrior king. He built Bamburgh Castle where he lived very happily with his beautiful wife, Bidda, and their two children, a handsome boy called Childe Wynd and a pretty girl called Margaret. When the children were still young, however, Bidda died and King Ida, feeling lonely, took a second wife, Bethoc. Unfortunately she turned out to be a spiteful witch.

Life soon became miserable for the children, for Bethoc not only resented Childe Wynd's friendship with his father, she became enraged every time someone complimented her on Margaret's good looks. Childe Wynd kept away from his stepmother as much as possible, practising with his sword and his bow, until he was old enough to leave the castle and seek his fortune over the sea. At last he was ready, and kissing Margaret farewell he promised her he would return as soon as possible. Then he mounted his horse and rode away.

King Ida was very sad that his son had left home, but Bethoc stirred things up, telling the King how rude Childe Wynd had been about him, and how he had bragged about what he would do when he was king. All of this was untrue, but it turned King Ida against his son. Meanwhile Margaret, missing her brother, was sad and withdrawn. The Queen treated her very badly and kept her shut away in a distant part of the castle, with no one to play with, and nothing to do.

One day, Margaret mentioned her unhappiness and loneliness to her father, but Queen Bethoc immediately lost her temper and sent the girl away. Then she smiled lovingly at King Ida, and offered him a drink of enchanted wine. After two sips, he forgot about his daughter's problems.

By the time Queen Bethoc came to find Margaret, she had decided how to punish the girl. The punishment would be terrible and would keep Margaret away from her father and out of the castle for good. If he asked, she would tell King Ida that his daughter had ungratefully run away. But it would not be the truth.

x x x

Time passed and tales began to spread of a terrible beast which was laying waste the countryside. It soon became known as the "laidly worm", or ugly serpent. It was a huge, greenish, slimy worm, and it could eat a pig in just two bites. It lived in a cave near Budle Sands, beneath a column of rock called Spindlestone Heugh, and for seven square miles all around the rock the grass was killed by its poisonous dribble and the slime which oozed from its skin. Children were not allowed out alone any more, for though it had not yet eaten a child, the laidly worm's jaws were easily big enough to swallow a ten-year-old. Every evening the local inhabitants brought the milk of seven of their best cows for a night-time drink, to prevent the worm from getting hungry at night, and so to protect their children and cattle. They would fill a hollow in front of the cave with the creamy new milk, and then run away as the disgusting beast emerged.

The country was terrorized. King Ida was not interested. He lived in his strong castle with his wicked wife, and brooded only occasionally on the absence of his children. Childe Wynd, winning glory abroad, heard rumours about the situation, and about the disappearance of his sister, and immediately decided to return. He had always suspected that his stepmother was a witch, and he took precautions just in case. He had his ship fitted with new masts of rowan, and silken sails, and when Queen Bethoc sent seven hags, friends of hers, to cause storms and sink him, their magic was powerless because of the rowan wood.

Childe Wynd landed safely on Budle Sands, and rode immediately to Spindlestone Heugh. He tied his terrified horse to the rock, and slipping slightly on the slime which covered the area outside the worm's cave, he drew his sword and prepared to attack the serpent. Behind him, his horse whinnied in terror. In front, the worm reared its loathsome head, and Childe Wynd forced himself to approach.

But strangely, as he attacked, the animal kept avoiding attacking him back. When he slipped and dropped his weapon and lay unarmed in a pool of dribble, the worm still failed to take advantage of the situation. On the contrary it crept close and nudged his hand with its snout. Controlling his feelings of revulsion, Child Wynd looked into the beast's eyes. He suddenly recognized his sister, under an awful magic spell, and forcing himself to ignore her appearance he kissed her three times. In a puff of smoke, the serpent turned back into his sister, Margaret, more beautiful even than she had been before.

They rode to King Ida's castle, and stopped in passing to take some holy water from a well. When they arrived, Queen Bethoc was waiting in terror, and when they sprinkled three drops over her, she turned into a huge scaly toad, and hopped away before King Ida's astonished eyes.

King Ida ruled Bernicia 547–559. He built the original Bamburgh Castle, though today's castle, still imposing, is mainly Victorian. Spindlestone Heugh is off the B341, and there is apparently still a shallow cave and a trough where the beast's milk used to be left.

To this day a huge toad can occasionally be seen crawling on Bamburgh sands before a storm.

OXFORDSHIRE

THE ROLLRIGHT STONES

AD 878

Throughout his youth in Denmark, Guthrum had heard stories about how exciting it was to come and raid England, and how easy it would be to invade properly and take over the whole country. So, as soon as he became King of the Danes Guthrum gathered an army and began to organize a major invasion of England.

All the Danes prepared their shields, spears, helmets and battleaxes. Having done that to Guthrum's satisfaction they set off in their special ships – long ones with oars along the side, and a carved figurehead at the front. After a long and rough journey they reached the shores of England. The Danes gratefully disembarked, their knees wobbling and their faces pale. Their mood matched their appearance, and it was only after they had burnt a few villages that they began to feel more themselves.

At that time England was split up into many small kingdoms, and all went well with Guthrum's invasion force until they reached the kingdom of Wessex, where Alfred was king. Now Alfred may have been a useless cook, but he was very brave and very obstinate. Even when Guthrum had defeated Alfred, Alfred was too obstinate to admit it and give in.

Once Alfred and his Anglo-Saxons had recovered from the shock of the Vikings' strange appearance, huge size and fierce fighting methods, they began to fight back, but the Vikings were still stronger and better armed, so Guthrum kept advancing, and Alfred kept retreating until one day a strange thing happened.

Alfred used to send out scouts to check how near Guthrum was to him, to make sure that Guthrum was not catching up with him, or planning some strange manoeuvre, but one day Alfred's scouts failed to find Guthrum's army! He sent more scouts out to check, but there was no sign of the Vikings anywhere.

Elfric was a small, blond boy, and he had proved to be one of Alfred's best scouts, partly because he knew the area well, and partly because he was so small that the Vikings had never noticed him. He came back to report to Alfred after searching in vain for Guthrum for several hours.

"Your Majesty," he said. "It's no use looking any more, they've just disappeared."

King Alfred was usually good-natured, but now he was worried, and when people are worried they are inclined to be cross. "Don't be so stupid, Elfric," Alfred snapped. "Armies don't just disappear! Didn't you see any trace of them?"

"The only thing I did see, sir," the boy replied sulkily, "was a lot of large new stones over by Little Rollright."

Alfred swore loudly in Anglo-Saxon. Why was this stupid boy

waffling on about stones when he, Alfred, had lost contact with a large and extremely hostile army?

Alfred remained worried and irritated for a whole week. Elfric remained sulky and upset for a whole week. Guthrum and his army remained lost for a whole week... and another week... and another week. At the end of the first week, Alfred and Elfric returned to their normal cheerful selves, and Alfred forgave Elfric, because after all he was (usually) his best scout. Guthrum's army, however, still remained lost, and after a few months it was assumed that they had returned secretly to Denmark.

X X X

What had happened was this. Guthrum had been advancing through the country, trying to catch up with Alfred and his army, so that he could beat them once and for all.

However Guthrum had problems with his army. He was a typical Viking – tall, blond, beefy and quite pleasant in spite of his plaits and his legwarmers. He was a jovial man who drank huge quantities of mead with great gusto, and who fought with even more relish. He was a great warrior, and when there was a battle on, Guthrum was in his element. Once off the battlefield, however, he was rather thick. He did not really know how to get on with his men except when he was fighting or telling rude jokes.

The problem with his army was that his men were fed up with just marching and looking for the enemy. They liked fighting, yes, but they also liked looting – stealing gold candlesticks from local churches, making people tell them where their money and treasure was hidden – and since they could not fight Alfred because he kept retreating, they could not understand why they could not at least stop and loot all the villages they passed? Guthrum hoped to catch up with Alfred and beat him once and for all, but this was not clear to his army. So Guthrum's men kept complaining and because Guthrum was not too bright he did not know how to stop them. What he should have done was to get rid of the troublemakers.

There were three. Their names were Hareth, Breca and Wiglaf. Hareth was large and burly, as broad as Guthrum himself, except his hair was not blond, it was dark. He had horrid bushy eyebrows which he had to trim every two months or else they would have covered his eyes. Not that that would have been any loss, because they were unpleasant eyes, fierce like a wild boar's, that shone red whenever he got into one of his terrible rages. Hareth was Guthrum's half-brother and he resented not being king. He would not have made a good king for, although he was a courageous fighter, he had a streak of cruelty which often made him act like a bully.

Breca was completely different. He was small where Hareth was enormous, cowardly where Hareth was brave, and cunning where Hareth was stupid. In fact, Hareth provided the strength, while Breca provided the brains. His eyes were hazel with a sneaky look about them, and whenever he thought of an evil plan he sniggered in a way which showed all his teeth.

The third of the troublemakers was Wiglaf. He comes last, because he was the least important of the three. He did what the other two told him, and might have been quite a pleasant person had he not fallen into such bad company. The others teased him unmercifully, giving him all the unpleasant tasks to do, which he was too silly to refuse.

Anyhow, these three troublemakers went round the ranks of the Viking soldiers as they were marching, and reminded them how hungry they were, and how thirsty, and how they had not had a good battle for ages, and how they had not been allowed to loot any of the villages, and other such things, until the army was so disgruntled that they refused to march any further that day. Since they had been marching for several days at a stretch and they were all tired, Guthrum agreed to stop, and only said, "My scouts tell me that near the top of this hill there is a clearing where we can camp."

Since they were already more than halfway up the hill the men agreed and a little while later they reached the clearing.

Until the Vikings came clattering in, Little Rollright Clearing was a calm, beautiful spot in the woods, the ideal place for a picnic. On one side of the clearing stood a little thatched cottage, in front of which a tiny, white-haired old lady sat sunning herself and stroking her cat who was snoozing quietly in her lap. When the Vikings entered, however, the quiet was shattered. The birds which had been feeding on the bread which the old lady had put down for them fluttered away, and the cat opened one green eye to stare lazily at the intruders.

The men ignored the old lady as they set up camp in a circle in the glade. Breca and Hareth watched as Wiglaf prepared their food. Suddenly Breca's beady eyes caught sight of the old lady and her cat. He nudged his friend.

"Hey, Hareth," he said. "Let's have some fun with the old biddy."

Hareth, his bullying nature aroused, agreed and the two men strolled over towards the cottage. Meanwhile Guthrum had been talking with his scouts.

"So you say Alfred is at Long Compton, the village just over the next rise?"

"Yes sir," the scout replied.

"And can I see it from the top of this hill?" Guthrum demanded. But he did not listen to the answer. He had noticed that Breca and Hareth were trying to take the old lady's cat away from her, so that they could tie Wiglaf's helmet to its tail. Guthrum strode over towards the troublemakers. Later he was to regret not having paid attention when the scout had tried to tell him that even from the very top of the hill, a mound hid the view of Long Compton.

"How many times have I warned you not to let this sort of thing happen?" he shouted. "I'll speak to you in a minute."

Hareth and Breca withdrew and stood apart from the other men. After a few moments Wiglaf joined his friends to find out what was happening, and the three stood huddled together muttering nasty comments about Guthrum.

The king meanwhile was apologizing to the old lady but she would not forgive him. She was a retired witch with a nasty streak, and when she fixed him coldly with her bright blue eyes, Guthrum began to feel very uncomfortable, even though he reminded himself that he was more than twice her size. Suddenly in a loud dramatic voice she cried out:

Seven long strides thou shalt take!
If Long Compton thou canst see,
King of England shalt thou be!

Silence fell on the glade. All the Vikings had heard her words, and were awed into silence.

Knowing that the scout had said that Long Compton, the village where Alfred was encamped, was just over the brow of the hill, Guthrum immediately took seven paces forward, crying:

Stick, stock, stone,
As King of England I shall be known!

To his dismay he could not see the village for a rise in the ground obstructed his view. So that was what his scout had been trying to tell him. Oh, why had not he listened? With a sudden feeling of foreboding, he started to run up the hill, but behind him he heard the old lady chuckle. "It won't help you, only seven steps!" Then she added in her special loud spell-casting voice:

As Long Compton thou canst not see,
King of England thou shalt not be;
Rise up, stick, and stand still, stone,

For King of England thou shalt be none;
Thou and thy men hoar stones shalt be
And I myself an eldern tree!

Guthrum's feet suddenly felt heavy and he could no longer move them. Standing above his men, where his short sprint had taken him, he turned to look back and was seized by an insane desire to laugh. Why, his men looked as though their feet were made of stone! As he watched, he saw the stony look spread up the knees of his soldiers, and felt the solid feeling spreading up his own legs. The feeling continued to engulf his body until eventually even his hair felt heavy. The old lady gave a cackle, and vanished with her cat and her cottage, leaving only a flourishing elder tree where she had been sitting. Soon the film of stone crept over Guthrum's eyes and he saw no more.

x x x

A few months later, when the kingdom had been settled and Alfred was restoring law and order, he and Elfric came up to Little Rollright Clearing with a select group of friends for a picnic. King Alfred now had time for picnics, for the enemy army had never been found.

Alfred was amazed at the stones, rough unhewn man-sized lumps of rock positioned in a clear circle, apart from a small group of three stones huddled together a short distance away and the one tall stone positioned above the others. After the picnic and a game of hide-and-seek around the stones Alfred, leaning against a stone, and panting gently because he was out of practice at playing hide-and-seek, said wonderingly, "How many do you think there are?"

Elfric, who was not puffed because he was always very fit, and another friend, set off to count them. They returned with conflicting opinions.

"There are 72," claimed Elfric.

"94," protested his friend.

"72."

"94."

"72."

"Quiet," bellowed King Alfred. Silence followed. "We will all count the stones. Everyone count the stones and return here in ten minutes."

Ten minutes later Alfred and his company reassembled and compared totals. Not one total agreed with another. Alfred decided to recount the stones, but this time he came up with a completely different total again. Exasperated, he declared, "The man will never live who shall count the stones three times and find the number the same!"

Having surprised himself and his friends with this profound statement, King Alfred the Great helped pack up the picnic and the company departed. Behind them the stone circle stood sadly and silently, as it does to this day. Occasionally, it is claimed, the Rollright Stones go down to the stream for the drink which they had not had time to enjoy before their fate befell them. And it is said that if you cut the branches of the surrounding elder trees they bleed witch's blood, not sap.

The Rollright Stones are just north of Chipping Norton off the A3400 at Little Rollright on the Oxfordshire/ Warwickshire border. Most of the rocks are in a circle. But there are three blocks together, on the far side of the privately owned field, and these are known as the Whispering Knights. The King Stone is on the other side of the main road, halfway up the hill, but its view of Long Compton is blocked by a mound known as the Archdruid's Barrow. The legends were

first written down in the 12th century, but the monument is thought to date from 1500 BC, the early Bronze Age.

   Picnics are no longer allowed but you can see the stones and try counting them.

OXFORDSHIRE

STARVED TO DEATH:
MINSTER LOVELL

1487

Francis Lovell was on the run. He had raised an army to fight the new king, Henry VII, and now it had been defeated. His remaining men scattered and Francis was left to make his own way, under cover of darkness and along hidden byways, to safety.

It was too difficult to reach the coast and as Francis considered his options, he decided to make for his own home. There was a secret chamber at Minster Lovell and there he could hide until the pursuit had died down.

At midnight the next day Timothy, the old steward at Minster Lovell, was startled to be awakened by a frantic whisper.

"Master Francis," he gasped, confused. "What are you doing here?"

"Timothy, you must hide me. The King's soldiers are hunting for me."

The old man sat up in bed, trying to rally his wits. "But where? What can I do? Surely this is the first place they'll look?"

"You remember the secret chamber, the hidden room? You showed me when I was a boy. Put me in there. You can bring me food when the coast is clear."

Timothy reached for a robe and tottered to his feet. Francis was dismayed to see how frail the old man had become. Together they tiptoed down the corridors to the secret room, where Francis was installed. Timothy went back to his room, but he was far too excited to sleep.

X X X

For several weeks Francis Lovell lay hidden. Timothy brought him food and water, and candles and books to read. The soldiers searched the house several times, but found nothing.

Then one day, disaster struck. Timothy had really retired from work several years ago because he was so old, but now he had to fetch and carry for his master once more. It was all too much. Moreover, there was the stress of making sure no one else in the household saw where he went or what he was doing. Trying to dodge into a doorway to avoid one of the other servants, Timothy tripped. The tray of food he was carrying slipped to the ground with a crash and as he fell the old man struck his head on the sharp doorframe.

The other members of the household, wondering where the old man had been going with so much food, thought he had become confused in his old age. As he lay dying he tried to say something, but no one understood.

Trapped in his secret room, which could only be opened from the outside, Francis Lovell waited in vain for Timothy to bring him his dinner... or his breakfast...

After the Battle of Bosworth in 1487, where the Tudor Henry VII took the crown and the Yorkist Richard III met his death, Richard's friend and chief minister, Francis Lovell, escaped to the continent. There he met a young man called Lambert Simnel, who claimed to be King Richard's nephew, and therefore rightful king. Lovell raised a small army and returned to England to try and put Lambert Simnel on the throne, but his forces were completely defeated.

Francis Lovell may have drowned after the battle, trying to escape across the river Trent. Anyway, he was never seen again and may have returned to his manor of Minster Lovell, on the banks of the beautiful River Windrush. In 1708 workmen repairing a chimney broke through into a secret room and found the skeleton of a man sitting at a table with a book, paper and pen in front of him. At his feet lay the body of his dog. As the fresh air reached the bodies they crumbled to dust.

The manor fell into disrepair during the eighteenth century, and is now a beautiful ruin. There is also a glorious dovecote. Minster Lovell Hall is 2.5 miles north-west of Witney, Oxfordshire.

The site is owned by English Heritage and is open to the public.

SOMERSET

DRAKE'S CANNONBALL: COMBE SYDENHAM

1583

Elizabeth Sydenham was to have married Sir Francis Drake. She was young and beautiful, he was rich and famous, and although her family did not like the marriage, she had managed to convince them. But just when she had persuaded them, Francis had announced he was leaving on another expedition. She was furious.

"Marry me first," she demanded.

"I can't," he replied. "There is too much to do. I have to organize four ships to sail to the other end of the world."

"For goodness' sake," she cried in a temper. "How hard can that be? You've done it before. Anyway, getting married doesn't take long."

"The Queen would be annoyed if I married you now," he explained, and tried to embrace her. She pushed him away.

"Well, I might not wait," she glowered at him, and stormed out of the room.

Francis shrugged his shoulders. He was sure she would wait. They had fallen in love a few years ago, but he was already married at the time, and it was only on the death of his first wife, that he had been free to court Elizabeth. She had never been interested in boring young men, but since she was old enough to be out of the schoolroom she had thought only about the rugged sailor who had gone all the way round the world and come back with the King of Spain's treasure. When he visited Sir George Sydenham, her father, Sir Francis (for he had been knighted after his historic trip) had soon been attracted to the beautiful and intelligent girl who always made sure she was present when he came to call. But now they had run into problems.

He sent her gifts to placate her, beautiful emeralds for a necklace and a golden goblet which had belonged to a Mexican king, but she refused to see him again before he left. Meanwhile his head was full of planning for his expedition. They needed to carry enough food and drink for eighteen months, and organizing the crews and the provisions took up all his time. When all was ready, he sat in his cabin waiting for the tide to turn and wrote to Elizabeth. He told her of his love for her, and begged her to have patience. "I will be back, and as soon as I touch land, I wish us to be married. Please have patience. Yours for ever, Francis."

She received his letter in silence, and read it with a lump in her throat. Of course she would wait.

However, as the months passed and grew into years, she grew bored and lonely. She received only one further letter, for he had no reliable method of sending news, and in her boredom she began to become very friendly with one of Francis's friends, John Hedge. He was, she told herself, rather dull, but very nice, and far more reliable than Drake. Her family were pleased with the new friendship. Soon Hedge proposed, and since she had now been waiting for two years with no word from Sir Francis, she accepted Hedge's proposal. The wedding was arranged.

Drake was in the Caribbean at the time, and by chance consulted a soothsayer, a wise old man. He told the sailor about Elizabeth's proposed marriage. Francis was furious. He returned to his ship in a terrible rage, and turning his guns towards England in a fit of temper, he loosed off a salvo of cannonballs aimed at Devon. When he had done that, he felt rather foolish, for he was many thousands of miles away, and cannonballs could only travel a few hundred yards. His men shook their heads sympathetically, but thought he had only himself to blame for leaving Elizabeth for so long. He gave orders to set sail for home immediately.

Meanwhile in England, the wedding of Elizabeth Sydenham and John Hedge was being celebrated. Elizabeth wore her best dress, trimmed with ribbons. Her hair was loose and garlanded with flowers. The priest had just reached the part of the service where he asks if anyone knows of any reason why the couple should not be married, when an ominous whistling noise was heard. The priest faltered to a halt, and everyone stood looking in terror at one another. Suddenly a hole was blown in the roof of the church porch, and a cannonball shot down and landed precisely between Hedge and Elizabeth.

Everyone stared at the smouldering ball. Elizabeth's dress was slightly singed. The priest fainted, and was later taken away with a suspected heart attack. After her initial shock, Elizabeth knew exactly what the cannonball meant, and cancelled the wedding. Hedge tried to move the cannonball but it was too heavy for him. It took five men to pick it up, and they carried it back to the hall at Combe Sydenham, where they placed it in a position of honour, and where Drake was greatly surprised to find it on his return from his travels. It looks very like a meteorite, but then perhaps cannonballs too are subject to great heat and pressure when they travel such long distances.

Combe Sydenham (Monksilver, Taunton) is five miles north of Wiveliscombe on the B3188. There is apparently a curse on anyone who tries to remove the "cannonball", but it is supposed to be lucky to touch it. In the past the farm men have carried the ball, which weighs over 50 kilograms, to the top of the deer park, but it always rolls back of its own accord. It is now kept in the Court Room.

Sir Francis Drake and Elizabeth Sydenham were married in 1585.

SUSSEX

ST DUNSTAN AND THE DEVIL:
MAYFIELD AND TUNBRIDGE WELLS

AD 961

Archbishop Dunstan had asked for a new church to be built in the little village of Mayfield. He was in charge of the whole of the church of England and adviser to King Edgar, as well as representing the Pope in England, so he was a very important man. Before he became so important, he had been a very good goldsmith and loved to make precious and beautiful objects. But now he hardly had any time for such matters, he was so busy with his official work.

When it was reported to him that the church at the village of

Mayfield was ready, he organized a special festival during which he could come and bless the church. Everything was ready, the villagers filled the church with flowers and put on their best clothes, and awaited the arrival of the Archbishop.

But when Dunstan alighted in front of the church he and his friends were dismayed. The new church had been built in slightly the wrong direction. Instead of facing east-west, it was slightly skewed.

Dunstan and his friends discussed what to do. The builders were very embarrassed about their mistake, and the villagers were upset that their new church was not perfect and maybe the Archbishop would not be able to bless it.

Then Dunstan came to a decision. He walked all round the church checking the angles and then, having worked out which corner to deal with first, he put his shoulder to the wall of the church, and pushed hard. The villagers looked on in amazement. Had the Archbishop gone mad?

Dunstan's face grew redder and redder with his efforts. Suddenly the church began to move. Dunstan grunted and continued to push, until the whole church had swung around the few feet needed to bring it into "true", facing the right direction.

Then he straightened up, dusted off his hands, and the ceremony was able to continue. The villagers were overjoyed. Not only was their church now perfect, but they had surely witnessed a miracle.

Dunstan himself was so pleased with the newly aligned church and the friendliness of the village of Mayfield in general, that he decided to buy a small house, just one room, with a smithy attached. In the house he could eat and sleep, and in the smithy he would have a forge with a fire, and all the tools for working as a smith. Most of the time he would be an important archbishop and statesman, and for a few days a month he would come and make golden objects, or even horseshoes and metal household items, for the local inhabitants. Both he and the villagers were delighted with the arrangement, and the important church officials grew used to his absences.

One day, when Dunstan was working hard making new horseshoes, he looked up to see a handsome stranger. He was tall and dark, and an unmistakable aura of evil emanated from him.

Without being told, Dunstan recognized the stranger. It was the devil himself, come to do harm to the village where the church had miraculously moved. As the stranger leapt forward to grab hold of Dunstan, the Archbishop reached behind him where his tongs were heating in the fire. He pulled them out and whipped them round as the stranger began to claw at him. He managed to snap the white-hot tongs closed on the devil's nose, and held on tight.

There was a tremendous scream of pain and fury that was heard throughout the county. Then with a massive jerk, the devil pulled himself free and leapt high in the air. He flew through the sky until he saw a cool stream, at the Pantiles in Tunbridge Wells, and there where the stream gushes forth, he landed and plunged his burning nose in to ease the pain.

Clouds of steam and sulphurous smoke rose up from the devilish nostrils, and he sighed with relief as the water eased his pain. Never again would he mess around with Mayfield Church or Archbishop Dunstan.

As abbot of Glastonbury, St Dunstan was renowned as a goldsmith, illustrator and musician. He became Archbishop of Canterbury in 961. He is usually shown in pictures holding the Devil with a pair of pincers by the nose.

In the convent of the Holy Child Jesus at Mayfield (follow the A267 out of Tunbridge Wells) there are some tongs which were supposedly used by St Dunstan, though they actually date from some 300 years too late.

At Tunbridge Wells the water still rises with clouds of steam and sulphurous smoke.

YORKSHIRE

THE PLAGUE STONE: YORK

14TH CENTURY

Guy helped to load up his father's cart with apples. He and his family lived just outside York and owned ten apple trees in a small orchard, as well as a little plot of land on which Guy's father grew vegetables. A neighbour had told them there was plague in the town, but that fruit and vegetables could be sold at high prices. As long as you could trade without coming into actual contact with the infected people or their money, there was a chance to make a good profit.

So that morning Guy and his father drove the laden cart up towards York. There was less traffic than usual on the road but still a few country people bringing their produce in for sale.

As the cart arrived outside the city walls they saw that the farmers were following a strange procedure. Guy and his father watched and then copied what the others were doing. They brought their cart up quite close to the walls and then unloaded the apples and left them in neat piles. Then they backed away to a safe distance. When they stopped, the townsfolk emerged and came over to the piles of fruit. Guy and his father watched as they selected what they wanted and then carefully dropped the money into a stone with circular holes filled with liquid.

Guy saw a little girl with tired-looking eyes come out from the town gates, select a few apples and then drop her coin into the liquid. She turned and looked over at them for a moment and there was a fleeting smile on her face. On impulse Guy waved and the girl waved back. She seemed to be wishing with all her heart that she could just leave the city and the dying people within it and run away with Guy to the clean air of the country-side. She took her apples and turned sadly back into the infected town. Guy wondered if her parents and brothers and sisters were all sick or dying, and whether she was the only one left. He hoped she would survive and offered up a quick prayer for her.

Then he and his father cautiously came forward and scooped the money out of the hollows of the stone. There was a strong smell of vinegar and Guy fervently hoped that it was true that vinegar acted as a disinfectant and would prevent them catching the plague and taking it back home with them. When all the apples were gone, he and his father returned home. Though they had made a good deal of money their mood was sombre.

The Plague Stone lies behind railings at the end of Burton Stone Lane. It has several circular holes in the top. When York was suffering from plague and no countryman in his

right mind would venture within the stricken city, this stone was an important meeting point between the possibly infected and the probably still healthy. The Lane used to lie just outside the town walls.

You can still walk around part of the town walls.

IRELAND

MALAHIDE CASTLE: DUBLIN

1976

Puck was worried. He was a very quiet, timid little ghost and normally he kept out of sight and out of everybody's way. But when he was worried, like now, he forgot to be careful.

The problem was he kept overhearing snippets of conversation, and the phrases he heard he did not like. It seemed that Malahide Castle, where he had lived for many centuries, was about to be sold. This was impossible! The castle had belonged to the Talbot family since 1185, 791 long years, and Puck had been there for most of that period.

The first Talbot, Richard, had been given the Lordship of

Malahide for promising to supply the King with one archer, with horse and armour, whenever the King should need them, for ever and ever.

While the Talbot lords had found fame and fortune on the battlefields of France and England, Puck (at that time still a live person) had been on duty at home on the battlefields of the castle. One evening, exhausted by several nights on watch, he had fallen asleep while on duty and awakened to find a troop of enemy soldiers approaching. The household had been aroused just in time and the enemy repulsed, but Puck had been unable to forgive himself.

Asleep on duty. A few more minutes and the castle would have found itself completely unprepared. Though everyone tried to console him, he became more and more depressed, until one night he took a cord and hanged himself by the neck from the Minstrels' Gallery, overlooking the Great Hall.

But he loved the castle so much that even after death he found he could not leave. Now bushy-bearded and wrinkled, the tiny little man, only a metre or so high, continued to dwell in the turret of the castle. No one bothered him, and he bothered no one. The inhabitants of the castle were even rather fond of him.

When the Talbots went out to fight at the Battle of the Boyne in 1690, to try and restore Catholic James to the throne which Protestant England had given to King William and Queen Mary, Puck watched worriedly from his turret. He saw fourteen members of the family ride off into battle, but he waited in vain for anyone to return. All fourteen perished that day.

But in spite of the terrible family losses at that battle, life had gone on in the castle and other Talbots had continued the tradition. Now, however, it seemed the building was to be sold and the last of the family had moved to Australia and could not keep up the house.

Puck was distressed. Would the ancient stones he loved be flattened to the ground? A young man sat in the Great Hall writing busily. Puck tried to make out what he was doing from the Minstrels' Gallery, but it was too far away. He crept down and came up behind the young man to see what he was doing. It seemed to be a list, a list of all the furniture and objects in the castle. An inventory. So it was true, they were preparing to sell everything.

A few weeks later, many people gathered in the hall and there was great toing and froing as the castle and its contents were auctioned. The County Council purchased the castle and opened it to the public. After a year of living on tenterhooks, Puck could relax. People came and looked round the castle, but his turret was undisturbed, and he soon got used to the guided tours.

The Talbot family lived in Malahide Castle from 1185 to 1973. In 1976, while preparing for the auction, a man from Sotheby's reported that while he was sitting down at the table in the Great Hall a wee silent man came and kept him company. Puck is another word for ghost.

The Castle is open to the public and is a short drive from Dublin's city centre.

NORTHERN IRELAND

GRAY'S PRINTING PRESS: STRABANE, COUNTY TYRONE

1760

Everyone in Strabane seemed to work in printing. There were printers for books and printers for pamphlets, printers for expensive books to keep for ever, and printers for cheap books that fell to pieces as you read them. At least ten businesses competed against one another.

John Dunlap had been surrounded by books for as long as he could remember. When he was still a young boy, maybe eight years old, he had been sent to work at Gray's Printery. The printing works was up an outside stairway and within the building was a paved yard. John had started as an apprentice sweeping out the yard, then as he grew more reliable and knowledgeable, he learnt to hammer in the wooden wedges that kept the letter type in the frame. Each word had to be created using the single metal letters, carefully selected and lined up with their fellows. Then the words were built up into phrases, sentences and finally pages.

Even when he was still only a boy, John had big ideas. He tried them out on his master, but the master was set in his ways and dismissed them with a shrug. If they all worked overnight, the boy said, they could produce a paper first thing in the morning so people could read all the latest news. And if they did not even bind the paper together like a book, but just folded the pages together it would be cheap and easy to prepare. But the old man just shook his head. A "newspaper" every day! It would be too much for people to read. And working through the night – what a bad idea.

When John was ten a letter came from his uncle in America, inviting him to leave Ireland and join him in Philadelphia. John's uncle was also a printer and a bookseller, and he was keen for the boy to work with him, and perhaps, if he was able, one day to take over the business.

John left Gray's Printery with few regrets and great hopes. He had learnt all they could teach him and now he needed a new place to let his ideas grow. He boarded the ship for the British colony of America, and sailed across the ocean with his head full of new ideas.

John Dunlap took over his uncle's business in Philadelphia in 1768. He developed it and soon launched America's first

daily newspaper. In 1776 he printed one of the most impor-
tant documents in American history, the Declaration of
Independence.

Gray's Printing Press is on the Main Street, Strabane and
still has a well-equipped printer's workshop (and an audio-
visual show).

SCOTLAND

THE TROJAN WINE BARRELS: EDINBURGH CASTLE

1341

The English held Edinburgh Castle, the most important fortress in all of Scotland, towering above the city. It was very difficult to capture, with its strong walls, atop high sheer cliffs. The English, smugly ensconced, ruled over the resentful Scots, but the soldiers kept within the castle and only ventured out into the city in large groups.

Sir William Douglas, Scottish lord of Liddisdale, and his cousin Archibald were determined to remove the English. But how could one retake the castle without risking death in the attempt?

THE TROJAN WINE BARRELS

At last, after much thought and planning, and after rejecting many ideas, they hit on a scheme which, although it required bravery, good acting, excellent timing and a great deal of luck, at least stood a chance.

Archibald disguised himself as a sea captain, claiming his ship had just anchored at Leith. He walked with a sailor-like roll and presented himself as a loyal subject of the English King Edward.

He requested an interview with the English governor of the Castle and told the guards at the gate that he carried a cargo of excellent French wines and would like to sell it to the garrison. The guards, easily convinced and eager to have some new stocks of wine brought in, immediately took him to see the governor, in his office in the heart of the Castle.

"My lord," Archibald Douglas began, bowing deeply, "my ship has just completed a very successful voyage to Bordeaux."

The governor's mood lifted. He was bored with his posting to this rainy, foggy northern outpost, far from London, and with nothing decent to drink.

Archibald continued. "I have several casks of excellent wine and other precious and tasty items on board, so I thought it my duty" (and here he bowed again) "to lay it all before your excellency that you may have first choice, before we offer it to the public."

He brought out a small flask of wine and handed it with a flourish to the governor.

"Hah," said the Englishman, tasting appreciatively. "Grapes from Burgundy. Delicious. It's been a long time since I've tasted such wine." He licked his lips and began to reminisce.

"I remember when we were fighting in France and we were encamped in the vineyards…"

Archibald stifled a yawn as the governor recited some tedious anecdotes about his past. But at last the man drained the small flask and made a decision.

"Send me a couple of hogsheads of this wine, and a selection of your other goods. When can you bring them?"

"Tomorrow morning, my lord."

Archibald left the castle trying to hide the grin on his face. When the guards enquired how the interview had gone, he told them he would be back in the morning with enough wine to make them happy.

That night, William and Archibald planned their ruse meticulously. Neither of them got much sleep that night.

Bright and early Archibald presented himself in his guise of sea captain, with twelve of his "crew", staggering under the weight of the casks, bales and boxes.

The guards, in anticipation of happy times, hastily drew back the bolts and threw open the gates. The laden men entered, but as the guards attempted to close the gates, the supposed seamen threw down their loads, blocking the gates. Each pulled out a broadsword from under his clothing and one blew a bugle loudly. 200 men, led by Douglas, who had been hidden behind carts and buildings a short distance away from the gates, rushed to the attack, swords flailing and voices upraised.

The English garrison was swiftly overthrown and the Scots soon feasted in the Castle on the French wine. Meanwhile the governor, confined to the darkest cell, had to be satisfied with water, and his life.

The Gatehouse is in the same position, but is no longer the original that Sir William Douglas would have seen in April 1341 when he made his assault. It is a late Victorian attempt from 1887–8 to make the Castle entrance look more imposing. The name of the sea captain is not known, though there is no reason why it might not have been Archibald Douglas.

SCOTLAND

THE BURIED HAND:
MARY KING'S CLOSE, EDINBURGH

1645

Under the streets of Edinburgh there lies another street. It is a dark and lonely street. No one lives there any more.

x x x

In 1645 many of the inhabitants of Edinburgh fell sick with the dreaded plague. Boils erupted on their bodies, first in their armpits and then all over, and they died in horrible agony. Medicine was useless and the doctors refused even to come and visit the sick.

When almost everyone on Mary King's Close had died, the authorities decided to brick up the street for ever. Who knew from where the plague came? Maybe the infection lurked in the very brickwork of the buildings themselves.

Only one man, Thomas Coultherd, refused to move. Born and bred on the street, he had only been outside the city walls once in all his life, and that had been a dreadful experience. His money had been stolen by a fellow traveller and he had had to return penniless back home. That had been enough for him. Since that day, many years before, Thomas had never left Edinburgh, and in fact rarely went beyond his own street.

And now the authorities were telling him he had to move. Already the greater part of his friends and neighbours had died or left, causing him great sorrow. At the thought of having to pack up and leave and face the hostile world anew, Thomas took to his bed. At first he wondered if he too had caught the plague, but he had none of the usual symptoms. He just had no reason to live. He lay in bed for a week without eating. Soon he grew too weak to leave even if he had wished it.

The deadline for the move approached and Thomas lay in bed, gazing uncaringly at the ceiling. When the city officials came to close up the street, they failed to notice the solitary inhabited house, amongst all the sick and dead. As they blocked off the last rays of daylight, Thomas whispered weakly, "Don't wall up our street... Don't wall up my house..." But there was no one left to hear him.

X X X

The street is called Mary King's Close, named after the daughter of Alexander King, lawyer and Advocate to Mary Queen of Scots, who inherited the property. It runs from the High Street under the City Chambers. During the nineteenth century the shops and workrooms northwards from the City Chambers were occupied once more, but in 1890 the Close was abandoned.

It is said you can sometimes still see Thomas' hand, just his hand, sticking through the wall, gesturing. If you visit the street, take a torch – and do not breathe in too deeply in case the germs still lurk... And above all, before you shake hands with any strangers, check that there is a body attached.

Tours of the site can be made only by prior arrangement with the City Chambers, tel: 0131 529 4318. Plague is spread by rats and is no longer found in Britain.

SCOTLAND

THE TREE OF CAWDOR: NAIRN

1370

The messenger arrived at the stronghold of Nairn and asked to see the Thane of Cawdor. He was tired and dusty, but he had good news and it was pleasant for once to be the bearer of good tidings. At least this time he would be made welcome and maybe even given some gold coins as a reward, instead of being shunned and sent hastily on his way, as usually happened if he brought bad news of death or lost battles.

He was one of the king's messengers and he carried with him a special licence. He patted his pocket to make sure he had it close to hand. His horse was taken off to the stables and he was offered a swift sip of ale, standing up, before being hurriedly shown into the presence of the third Thane of Cawdor.

"You bring news?" enquired the Thane instantly. The messenger toyed with the idea of retorting that no, he had merely ridden several days across some of the most inhospitable terrain in the kingdom just for fun, but he thought better of it. Clearly the news was important to the Thane and it would be cruel to keep him on tenterhooks. He held out the slim packet and bowed deeply.

The Thane ripped open the seal and eagerly spread out the sheet within. His eyes lit up as he read the contents. Then, as the messenger had hoped, the Thane told his steward to see that the bringer of good news was well cared for, and hurried away to tell his wife.

"Mary," he cried as he entered her chamber. "Mary, we have the royal licence! We may build our own castle, and fortify it in case the king should have need of a strong arm in this region. We have been selected!"

He almost danced with joy, for it was indeed an honour. His wife, quiet and placid, looked happy because he was happy. Still, she said the right things and he was in such a good mood that they feasted all evening at the stronghold of Nairn.

But when his friends asked him exactly where he would build his castle, the Thane fell silent. He had not yet made precise plans and he had no real idea which site to select, whether near to Nairn or far away. The king had not been specific, and the Thane had so far concentrated all his hopes on getting the licence, without considering the details. Now he had the licence, he had no idea what to do with it.

Late that night he discussed the problem with his wife. "Don't worry," she said to him. "You'll sort it out. Let's go to sleep. The night will bring good advice."

And it did. The Thane of Cawdor fell almost immediately into a deep sleep, worn out by the excitement of the day. He began to dream a vivid, detailed dream. In the dream a dusty messenger galloped into the hall, flung off his cap and slid from his horse.

"My Lord," he shouted, and everyone in the hall fell quiet and listened. "Load up your favourite donkey, Jennifer, with the chest of gold hidden under your bed, let her loose and follow her wherever she goes. Where she stops to rest, there the king's licence decrees you shall build your castle."

The Thane of Cawdor started out of his sleep, and sat up abruptly in bed. How did the messenger know he had a favourite donkey and that her name was Jennifer? He was rather embarrassed about being fond of a mere donkey, so this was not widely known. And then again, how did the messenger know about the chest of gold under his bed? The Thane of Cawdor was deeply troubled about how the messenger in his dream could have known these things.

He decided it must therefore be true. He should follow the dream messenger's advice. Resolved on this course of action, he rolled over and slept soundly once more, this time until morning.

After breakfast the next day he called for his servants and ordered them to carry down the chest from under his bed and load it onto the donkey. The servants looked perplexed, but the Thane did not feel like explaining. It had been bad enough telling his wife what he meant to do.

Then he packed a hunk of bread and cheese and a flask of water, took Jennifer's bridle and set off. Once outside the walls of Nairn, he stood in front of Jennifer and explained the situation to her (having first checked that no one was listening). Then he loosened the animal and prepared to follow wherever she might wander.

Jennifer was delighted. It was the thistle season, and the spiky blue flowers were just ripe, exactly as she liked them. Grass and hay are all very well, but what a donkey really loves are pointy, bristly thistles, which no one else wants to eat anyway. So Jennifer wandered hither and thither, from blue clump to blue clump, chewing and munching to her heart's content. True, the box on her back was heavy, but it was wonderful to be able to go wherever she wished and stay for however long she wanted.

Behind her the Thane of Cawdor plodded along. He had long since eaten his provisions, but he had managed to refill his water flagon at a passing stream where Jennifer stopped to drink.

At last, as evening fell, the tired donkey looked for somewhere to spend the night. Stuffed full of thistles she felt sleepy, and suddenly spying a hawthorn tree on a small hill above the river she lay down to spend the night there. Though she and the Thane had travelled many circuitous miles that day, they were only about five miles south-west of Nairn as the crow flies.

The Thane tethered Jennifer in case she should wander off with his gold during the night and then lay down by her side. He was weary but content. The site looked promising, so far as he could make out in the gathering gloom.

The next morning he returned to Nairn to announce his decision. But as he told his wife about the site Jennifer had chosen, a new thought suddenly struck him. Should he cut down the tree and build exactly where it had been?

He tried to remember the detail of his dream. The more he thought about it the more sure he became that, at least in the dream, the tree had not been destroyed. On the contrary, the new castle's square keep had been built around it, with the tree still growing up out of the floor and on through the ceiling.

The Thane's wife shrugged her shoulders when she heard about his plans. "Yes, dear," she said.

X X X

Cawdor Castle is open to the public. You will find it on the B9090, four miles south-west of Nairn. The building is surrounded on three sides by a moat, with the Cawdor Burn on the fourth. The hawthorn tree can still be seen, in the Thorn Tree Room, and tests have shown it to date from around 1370, the date of the foundation of the castle.

SCOTLAND

EDIN'S HALL: BERWICKSHIRE

The King of Scotland's daughter disappeared while playing in the forest one day. The king was so upset that he became withdrawn and unable to deal with the problems of his subjects.

One of these subjects, a widow with three sons, was too poor to pay her rent. She had no choice but to send one of her sons, Ben, away to seek his fortune. The night before he left, Ben gave the second brother his favourite knife, and said to him, "As long as the blade remains bright I am all right. If it turns rusty and dull, I am in trouble."

After travelling for several weeks Ben came to a castle, and asked at the back door whether he could stay the night. The woman in the kitchen said the castle belonged to Red Edin, a famous and unpleasant giant. Nevertheless she made him welcome, and sat him down with a bowl of soup.

Suddenly Red Edin himself entered, three-headed, huge and terrible. His hair was long and wild and flamed scarlet. His face was gnarled and ugly and the look in his eyes was mean. Without introducing himself he immediately asked three questions: "Did men live in Scotland or Ireland first? Was man made for woman, or woman made for man? Which was made first – man or beast?"

Even if his mouth had not been full of soup, Ben would not have known the answers, and without further ado the giant hit him on the head with a mallet, and the boy turned into a pillar of stone.

Back at home, the second brother, Tim, noticed the blade of the knife had become rusty and set off, first giving his own favourite knife to the third brother with the same instructions, "If the blade turns rusty and dull, I am in trouble."

But exactly the same fate befell Tim.

The last brother, Henry, noticed the knife blade had become dull and rusty. He informed his distraught mother that he must now leave in search of his fortune and of his brothers. He too then set off.

On the way, he met an old and tired lady. He felt sorry for her, and offered to share his last slice of bread with her. Then he helped her to carry her bag. They chatted as they walked along and Henry told her of his brothers' disappearance.

"Now listen to what I say," said the old lady stopping in the middle of the road. "I'm sure as can be that those brothers of yours have gone to Red Edin's castle. I used to know Edin when he was a young giant, and a nasty piece of work he was, and still is. You mark my words, he's going to ask you some questions, and if you can't answer them, you've had it. He always used to do this and he's the sort that doesn't change once he's set in his ways." And she nodded sagely. Henry waited with bated breath.

"What will the questions be?" he prompted, as she seemed to have lost the thread of her tale.

"Oh, I can't remember," she said, shaking her head.

Henry was disappointed. They walked on together a little further, and then, just as they were parting, the old lady said, "But I do remember the answers. I'll tell you and you try and memorize them, for you never know they might come in useful."

She told him the answers, but they did not make much sense without the questions. Henry tried to just remember them, the way he memorized meaningless things he did not quite understand at school. He said goodbye to the old lady and handed her back her bag. She wished him well and tottered off down the road.

Soon Henry arrived at the castle, where the old woman in the kitchen welcomed him in and offered him a bowl of soup.

No sooner had he started to eat, than Red Edin entered, three-headed, huge and terrible, his hair like a flame on his ugly head. Without further ado, the giant again asked his three questions: "Did men live in Scotland or Ireland first? Was man made for woman, or woman made for man? Which was made first – man or beast?"

Henry, warned by the old lady, had swallowed his mouthful, and was ready with the answers. The giant was so surprised at receiving the correct answers that his attention was distracted. By the fire lay an axe used to chop wood for the fire. Henry grabbed hold of this and since one of his main jobs at home was cutting the wood for the fire, he was very skilled with an axe. Within seconds, all three of Edin's heads were off.

Henry's brothers were instantly released from their spell. Together the three brothers opened the dungeons, where they found many prisoners, including the King of Scotland's daughter. All were released, Henry married the princess and happiness returned to the kingdom.

But once Henry had used the answers to the questions they went completely out of his head, and now no one knows the answers.

Edin's Fort is a tumbling-down ruin which dates back to the second century AD. Traditionally a giant's lair, its walls were five metres thick.

You can find it by following the A6112 from Preston to Grantshouse. 2.5 miles along this road, there is a sharp bend to the right. Opposite this is a lesser road, to the left. Walk down here until you come to a small burn (Otterburn). Continue along the south of the burn and cross a flimsy bridge. The water splits here; follow the burn to the right, go up the hill and at the top you will find Edin's Fort and Broch. The ruin is just over a mile from the A6112.

SCOTLAND

THE SLEEPING BEAUTY
IN THE TOWER: ST ANDREWS

1860

Theo, Felix and Pym had been down to the harbour to have a look at the fishing boats and were returning home. They had half an hour before their supper, so they dawdled along as they walked the length of the cathedral wall.

A couple of workmen were supposed to be fixing it. For centuries the wall had been covered in ivy, and the stonework underneath had suffered as a result. Now they were supposed to be hacking back the creeping tendrils and trying to fix the damage beneath. It was not a very pleasant job for the ivy was full of insects, some of them biting ones, and the more they uncovered, the more they had to do. The little aerial roots had eaten deep into the mortar of the stonework and in some cases the stones simply fell out with the ivy, leaving gaping holes. The workmen, depressed at their task, had downed tools and gone home early.

"Look," said Felix. "There's a bird's nest up there. Do you think there are any eggs in it?"

Theo, his head full of thoughts of climbing rigging and sailing the seven seas, offered to scramble up and have a look. The ivy was old and strong and offered ample hand-holds, while his feet found their grip on the crumbling masonry of the cathedral wall. Suddenly a strand of ivy came away from the wall. His feet kicked for a new foothold, but the stone he had trusted became dislodged and he tumbled backwards.

He did not fall too far – his feet had been at the other boys' eye level – and luckily he landed on a patch of soft grass. But the other boys, after checking briefly that he was not injured, had turned their attention to the wall. The stone which he had knocked out lay on the ground. It had left a hole, a hole through which one could peep at something hidden for centuries.

The boys looked at one another. Then Felix stepped forward to peep through the hole. He pressed his eye to the gap. His friends waited, holding their breath.

Pym looked around while he waited for Felix to tell them what he could see. He realized they were actually standing in front of a kind of tower, built into the wall. It was solid and square, not very tall, and formed part of the main bulk of the wall, beyond the lighthouse turret. On the other side of the wall would be the Cathedral and all the land belonging to the church. Suddenly Felix gave a cry and fell back.

"What is it, what did you see?" asked the boys, but Felix could only shake his head, too terrified to talk yet. Still sitting on the grass, he managed to crawl a few paces further from the wall, putting some distance between himself and the frightening thing he had seen.

The boys waited. Soon he had recovered a little. "It's... it's a girl... a body..."

"What was it? A ghost?" asked Theo worriedly. His older brothers had told him tales of a White Lady who was supposed to haunt the walls, somewhere round about here, and suddenly seeing his friend's shock, it all came back to him. His granny too had told him how the fishermen used to run past the walls on their way to the harbour, afraid to linger in case they saw the White Lady up on the ramparts. He shifted uneasily.

"No," Felix shook his head. "A real one. In a coffin."

Pym took a deep breath. He stepped up to the wall, and bravely put his eye to the opening. He was terrified that something would grab him and drag him through the gap. As he stared wide-eyed through the hole, he gradually became accustomed to the dark.

He could just make out a square room with a door at the far side. Around the walls lay ten wooden coffins, undamaged, with pointed lids. One lid had slipped off and rested on the chamber floor, next to its coffin. Lying inside, like a princess asleep waiting for her prince, was the body of a beautiful young girl, perfectly preserved. She was dressed in white, and her long black hair lay draped over her shoulders. She wore white gloves of smooth shiny material, which came up past her elbows.

Pym was very frightened, but he remained at his post, fascinated by the scene, and by the girl's quiet beauty. Then he stepped down. Felix still looked shocked. Theo did not dare to look. In silence they replaced the missing brick and covered all signs of their discovery. Then they went home for a very subdued dinner.

Years later, when he was a very old man, Pym heard the story of the Sleeping Beauty in a book for children. He thought back to the day he had seen the girl in the tower. The memory of her sad beauty had never left him.

The cathedral wall was built by Priors John and Patrick Hepburn early in the sixteenth century. The Tower was opened up in 1868 when a Mr Hall discovered ten well-preserved coffins, one of which contained a girl dressed in white. The coffins were probably of oak, and ridge-topped indicating they were of very early origin, perhaps between the fifth and thirteenth centuries. Some reports speak of twelve attendant mummy skeletons, decked out as at a feast. Others report that these attendant skeletons were clearly of different periods. No one knows who the people were, but it is assumed they were inhabitants of the castle.

By 1888, the room had been vandalized. The college museum holds a dainty embalmed foot of a girl, which may originally have come from the tower.

It is said a White Lady haunts the cathedral walls at that part, but the identity of the Sleeping Beauty remains a mystery.

St Andrew's Cathedral and Priory are at the far north-east corner of the town, between the harbour and the ruined castle. The "haunted" tower is situated behind the twin towers on the Cathedral wall. The Cathedral is open all year.

SCOTLAND

GREYFRIARS BOBBY: EDINBURGH

1858

Bobby was only a puppy, and like most puppies he ate things he should not. He ate John Gray's slippers. He ate the brim off John Gray's hat. He chewed the leg of John Gray's chair, so that when he sat on it, it wobbled. But when John turned to scold Bobby, the puppy looked up at him with such an innocent face that John could not bring himself to be too stern.

Bobby made puddles everywhere when he was very young. He did them in the middle of the kitchen, and by the back door when he could not get out in time. He even did one under John's bed which John only noticed when it began to smell bad.

Bobby grew up a little and began to behave better. The little dog accompanied John Gray wherever he went. He was not really a farmer's dog, for he was small and little use at herding sheep or attacking thieves. At first people laughed at John for taking his little dog everywhere, but very soon they grew used to him and came to expect the little shadow to follow him everywhere, whether in the pub, the street, or the field.

x x x

One day John felt unwell. Perhaps he had caught a chill, and being old and living in a very cold house and not eating properly, he grew sicker and sicker. One morning, when Bobby jumped up on the bed to wake his master, as he did every day, John Gray did not wake up. Bobby could not understand. He whined, he nudged his master, and eventually when there was no response, he lay down by his master's hand and just waited.

When John's friends, worried at not seeing him for lunch, came to knock on his door, they found him lying there cold, his faithful dog patiently waiting.

"Poor little thing, he doesn't understand," said Bill, John's best friend. "I'll take him home with me and look after him."

He scooped up the little dog and tried to carry him out, but Bobby would not go. He wriggled and wriggled until they had to drop him. Then he lay back down next to his master. They kept trying to pick him up and in the end he became quite nasty and had to show his teeth and growl before they would leave him alone.

"All right," said Bill. "Wait until old John is buried. Then he'll understand."

But he was wrong. John Gray was laid to rest in the graveyard at Greyfriars Church, but little Bobby, who had followed the coffin all the way from his home to its last resting place, would not leave. He lay by his master's grave, waiting until he was needed.

John Gray's friends watched worriedly for a while and then were forced to go about their business. When the church clock struck twelve, Bobby got to his feet and trotted along to the pub where John always went at noon. He waited patiently in line and was pleased when the landlord, warned of his small client's presence below the counter by the other customers, greeted him. "Hello, Bobby. Good to see you. Your usual?"

And without further ado the landlord went off to prepare Bobby's usual meal of meat scraps and gravy. Lunch finished, Bobby went back to his master.

The next day was the same. The churchwarden put down a water bowl for him, and the landlord was ready with his lunch.

John's friends were amazed at the dog's behaviour. For a few months they tried to entice him away, but soon they realized that it was useless. Bobby was going to stay with his master for ever.

Bobby lived by John Gray's grave for fourteen years. On his death he was buried near to his master. A fountain was erected in Candlemaker Row, just outside Greyfriars Church, for the benefit of both people and dogs. At the foot is a basin for dogs to drink from, with taps above for people. On top is a statue of the little dog. The inscription reads "A tribute to the affectionate fidelity of Greyfriars Bobby. In 1858 this faithful dog followed the remains of his master to Greyfriars Churchyard and lingered near the spot until his death in 1872."

SCOTLAND

BONNIE BETTY BURKE: SKYE

1746

Flora MacDonald was 24, not very tall, with dark brown hair, high cheekbones, and a gentle smile. She could sing Gaelic songs and play the spinet so beautifully it made you cry. Her family was important in the locality, but her father had died when she was only a baby. They lived on a desolate island called

South Uist, in a low thatched cottage with small windows. Behind her house lay the rough mountains of Beinn Mhor and Hecla and on the whole island there were no towns and scarcely even any villages, just small isolated farms.

Bonnie Prince Charlie was only two years older than Flora, but his life in Europe and on the battlefields of mainland Scotland and England seemed a million miles away. After years of planning in France, he had launched his campaign for the thrones of both Scotland and England. It had begun so well. He had no sooner arrived in Scotland on the first stage of the campaign than he had taken Edinburgh and routed the English. But then came the disastrous Battle of Culloden.

The Duke of Cumberland had won a great victory there, beating Charles Stuart (Bonnie Prince Charlie) and his friends conclusively. After the battle he had ordered all wounded men to be cold-bloodedly slaughtered, and for this he became known as Butcher Cumberland.

Meanwhile, Prince Charles' friends had dragged him away from the battlefield.

"Your life is precious," they said to him when he tried to argue. "If you are killed that's the end of the Jacobite rebellion. You must save yourself."

Finally he agreed, though reluctantly, and they led him to where a fresh horse was tethered. Then began a mad gallop to the coast, and endless journeys in small boats. Butcher Cumberland's men followed close behind.

In Benbecula on South Uist in the Outer Hebrides the Prince paused for breath. Friends brought him food and fresh clothing. They also brought news. They assured him he had been right to escape from the battlefield when he did. They wanted to get him back to France, but the Royal Navy was searching for him and prevented the French ships from coming in to pick him up.

Prince Charles was forced to sleep and eat rough, hiding out in the wilds. The height of luxury was a gamekeeper's hut, while the Navy ships patrolled past, seeking their quarry and preventing his rescue.

A reward of £30,000 was placed on his head and someone must have given a hint of his whereabouts, for a troop of government soldiers arrived. The net was beginning to tighten. It was time to escape.

x x x

When the soldiers were less than a mile away the Prince and his friends had to scatter. They destroyed their boat so the pursuing soldiers would find no clues, and set off. On 20 June 1746 Prince Charles Stuart met Flora MacDonald for the first time.

She was brought from her home by her stepfather who told her he needed her urgently at a friend's house. When she came in, she was introduced to the Prince and gasped in surprise. There had been rumours he was hiding nearby, and everyone knew about the soldiers, but to actually meet him... He gave her no time to think and immediately told her about his brilliant idea.

"It's very simple," he explained. "I shall dress as your maid. You will order me about, and I will help you to put your hair up and carry your bag, and so we will escape."

Flora was very dubious. The Prince was tall, and looked unmistakably like a man. Being brought up a Prince he also had a regal way with him. But he was her prince, and handsome, and when he looked at her with a mixture of arrogance and pleading in his blue eyes, she could only agree.

She left to collect some clothes for him. On the way, she was stopped by some soldiers and held overnight, so close and so suspicious was the pursuit. The next day she was late to the meeting place and found the Prince sitting on a large rock as arranged, but hungry and sick with worry.

She took him quickly to a friendly neighbour's barn, and there she brought out the costume. The Prince modestly insisted that he keep his breeches and waistcoat on, for which Flora was quite grateful. But then there were many layers to put on. First came a quilted petticoat, to be worn under a gown of calico material patterned with lilac flowers. On top came a white apron, and to hide it all a dark cloak with a large hood. Flora dug in her bag and pulled out a large white cap which, when pulled forward a little, hid most of his face. There were also stockings with blue velvet garters to hold them up, and shoes. If the situation had not been so desperate they would have had great fun. Even so they laughed at the finished maid.

"I shall call you Betty," Flora said. "How do you like that?"

The Prince considered. "Betty Burke," he amended. "And I should like to be Irish, for I can do the accent very well."

"Good. And you are clumsy at housework, but very good at spinning."

He grinned, and then turned to pick up his gun. "You can't keep that!" she cried. "A maid would never have a gun."

He was very unhappy, but she took it and stored it away in her bags, leaving him only a short heavy cudgel from which he refused to be parted.

They set off and travelled by foot to a neighbour who offered them a good mutton dinner. As they were finishing off their meal, news came that General Campbell had landed nearby with 1,500 men. They thanked their host and set off for the beach where a boat was supposed to be waiting.

And so, late in the evening, they pushed off from Long Island to sail over the sea to Skye. It was raining at first, though it eased off later. They dared not raise the sail on the little boat for fear of being seen by patrolling warships. The boatmen rowed hard, and as dawn rose they saw that they were lost in a thick mist. The boat drifted for a while, and everyone stared anxiously through the swirling fog to try and see something, anything. Suddenly they made out a row of black cliffs. One boatman thought it might be Waternish Point, but suddenly they realized it was Dunvegan Head, on the right island, but too far to the west, and belonging to the MacLeods, who were very likely to turn the Prince over to the English as soon as he set foot on land. The exhausted boatmen rowed as hard as they could away from those dangerous cliffs.

By now it was Sunday morning, and as they passed a beach, two militiamen spotted them and raised their guns to shoot. A bullet whistled past Flora's hat, and everyone ducked and continued rowing as fast as possible.

A few hours later, with no one apparently chasing them, they drew into a little half-hidden beach which is still called Prince Charles's Point, on Trotternish Peninsula, in the north-west of Skye, near the home of Sir Alexander and Lady Margaret MacDonald.

Betty was told to wait on the hills just outside Sir Alexander's house, while Flora went in to check that the coast was clear and to tell Lady MacDonald of their arrival. To her horror, she discovered that a party of soldiers had just been checking the house, and that Lieutenant Alexander MacLeod, the officer, was even at that moment having dinner there.

Flora kept her head, and refused to panic, though she was tired and wet from the long sea journey. She asked a maid to take a message in to Lady Margaret to say she had called. Lady Margaret, greatly excited, excused herself to the Lieutenant and came out.

"What shall we do?" she cried, wringing her hands.

"Just stay calm," said Flora. "You organize a servant to go and collect the Prince – just tell them it is my maid, Betty. Be sure not to mention anything about the Prince. I will go and talk to the officer."

So Flora walked quietly in and chatted to Lieutenant MacLeod about the weather and his children, while Lady Margaret sent someone to bring the princely maid down from the hill.

As the officer was saying his farewells with his soldiers at the front of the house, Prince Charles was entering at the back. Lady

Margaret's servants were shocked at the behaviour of a maid who refused to carry her own baggage, and who hoicked up her skirts in an indelicate way to ford a river. But that night the Prince slept in a bed, a rare luxury which he greatly appreciated.

The next day he threw away Betty's clothing and reappeared as a Prince. His farewell to Flora was warm. She had saved his life, at considerable risk to her own. The soldiers were no longer closely on the scent; they thought he was on a faraway island. A few months later he managed to catch a ship to France.

Flora herself was captured a few weeks later, and taken as a prisoner to London. After a year she was released, but by then Bonnie Prince Charlie was long gone from Scotland, back to Europe where he was to stay for the rest of his life.

The disastrous battle of Culloden took place in April 1746 where the Jacobite army of Prince Charles Edward Stuart (also known as the Young Pretender or Bonnie Prince Charlie) was bloodily defeated by the Duke of Cumberland.

The Flora MacDonald Monument, an eight-metre Celtic cross erected as a memorial stone, (blown down in 1873 and re-erected more firmly in 1880) is in Kilmuir Kirkyard, east of the A856, near the north end of the Trotternish peninsula on the Isle of Skye. In South Uist, Milton, where Flora was born in 1722, there is a cairn with an inscription, a few hundred yards off the main road.

Flora was described by Boswell, a famous diarist, as "a little woman of a genteel appearance, and uncommonly mild and well-bred." After emigrating to North Carolina with her husband, the laird of Kingsburgh, she later returned to Skye and is buried there. She died in 1790, aged 68, and 3,000 people came to her funeral.

SCOTLAND

THE LOCH NESS MONSTER

When I was only a very young monster, I swam away from my family to explore. We lived at that time in the open sea, but played around the rocky shore. That day I found a particularly interesting cave. It was deeper and longer than most of the coastal caves and I swam and swam into its depths. The current was strong and I had to work hard to make any progress forwards.

Instead of reaching a dead end, I came out of the cave into a wonderful lake. I explored this lake for a few hours, but when I tried to find my way back to the open sea and the rest of my family, I could no longer find the opening to the cave.

And so I have lived for many years in this lake, which I have come to regard as my home. I was a little lonely at first, but I had been a solitary sort of monster, and once I became accustomed to the idea of living here, and stopped hunting for the cave entrance, I was happy again. I had been ready to leave my parents anyway, and I had always found the rest of the herd fairly boring.

I was first spotted in the sixth century when I foolishly tried to attack a man called St Columba. I don't know what came over me, he just annoyed me and I was at a loose end that day, and had failed to catch a good fish for my lunch. Anyway as I tried to bite him, he shouted at me, and so frightened me that I dived back below the water and was afraid to come back for many hundreds of years.

When I did surface and have a look around I was not usually spotted, but all that changed in May 1933 when I came up for a bit of fresh air and a little splash around. As I looked to the shore I could see a couple of people pulling over to the side of the road in a strange four-wheeled contraption and pointing towards me.

I went back under as quickly as I could and, leaving streams of bubbles and foam behind me, plunged back to the depths where I usually live.

The next time I was seen, in 1952, was a complete disaster. I had no sooner popped up my head and back than I was hit by a very fast boat. The boat smashed into tiny pieces all round me, and I had a terrible headache, and bruises over my back. I think the pilot of the boat was killed, for which I was very sorry.

A few years after that awful experience, I realized that I had become famous. It seemed as though every time I put my head out to have a look around, someone took a picture of me. I decided I should stay at the bottom of the loch for several years to let the interest die down. So all during the 1960s, while people were scientifically trying to photograph me or film me, I just kept away.

Then they sent down a strange little yellow submarine. I hid in one of the caves near the banks of the lake, or sank into the mud at the bottom whenever I heard it approaching. It never caught sight of me, I'm sure, and after a few months it got fed up and I never saw it again.

Nowadays I am more careful. I only come up at night, or in the day during a rain shower, when there is usually no one about. And I limit my appearances to only one or two a year. I'm quite shy really.

St Columba made one famous journey north among the Picts when he visited King Bridei at his court near Inverness, and it was on his way there, on the River Ness, that he confounded a great water-beast who rushed at him "with gaping mouth and with great roaring". The story is related by Adamnan, abbot of Iona around 560 and is the first mention of the Loch Ness monster.

You can visit the many shores of Loch Ness with ease. The A82T runs from Inverness to Fort Augustus and on to Fort William, and there are two Nessie Exhibitions at Drumnadrochit on the way.

Monster enthusiasts have speculated that Nessie may be a plesiosaur, a giant newt, a huge seal, a swarm of salmon, an otter, a roe deer with antlers swimming along or a giant eel. In spite of years of watching and waiting, no one has managed to produce incontrovertible visual proof of the existence of a monster. What do you think?

WALES

BEDDGELERT: GWYNEDD

13TH CENTURY

Prince Llewelyn the Great was up early that morning. He usually was, for the baby woke him just as the sun rose each day, and the child's chuckles – which usually turned to loud bawling within a few minutes – could be heard emanating from the nursery all over the castle. But that day, Llewelyn had decided to go hunting, so he was not unhappy to be roused early from sleep.

He dressed and called his men to get the horses and dogs ready. The Prince's favourite hunting dog, Gelert, was already frisking about his knees, getting in the way, excited about going out for a day with his master.

But no sooner had they left the castle grounds, than Gelert suddenly stiffened, and turning, ran back to the castle. This was extraordinary behaviour, for the dog usually tried to keep close by his master's side. Prince Llewelyn sent a man back to get the dog, and the party waited. The luckless servant soon emerged, dragging a reluctant hound by his leash. Llewelyn had a word with the dog, who wagged his tail enthusiastically, but no sooner had he been let off the leash than he disappeared back inside the castle. Short of dragging him along on his haunches all day, there was no alternative but to leave the irritating animal behind. Prince Llewelyn, puzzled and rather annoyed, shrugged and put the incident behind him.

x x x

They had a splendid day's hunting, and returned to the castle tired, hungry and happy. At the gate stood a joyful Gelert, tail wagging furiously, leaping up at Prince Llewelyn's elbow with excitement. The party suddenly fell silent as everyone noticed that Gelert's jaws were dripping with blood. What had he killed or eaten? The party looked at one another in perplexity.

Suddenly the Prince caught sight of his son's nursemaid, flirting with her boyfriend, one of the grooms, in the courtyard over by the well. Realizing his baby must have been left unattended, Prince Llewelyn feared the worst.

Running faster than he had ever moved before, he raced up to the nursery, only to see a dreadful sight. The cradle lay overturned, the furniture was shattered, there was blood spattered over the walls. There was no sign of the baby.

"My son," cried Prince Llewelyn.

With fury and hatred in his heart, the Prince turned to the dog who stood by his side, his tail still wagging happily, his grey nose stained with blood. He pulled out his sword, and with a sob plunged it through Gelert's heart. His men, who had followed him up, stood at a distance, respecting his sorrow, and aghast at the unhappy events.

Suddenly a small gurgle was heard. Everyone froze. Another chuckle, unmistakably babyish. Prince Llewelyn walked very slowly, as though his legs were made of something heavy and immovable, into the room. The baby gurgling came thick and fast, and seemed to be coming from under the destroyed cot. The Prince lifted the debris out of the way, and there lay his son, unharmed in the mess of bedding.

A few feet away, its throat torn out by the brave dog, lay an enormous grey wolf. How it had got in, no one could understand, but Gelert had prevented it from doing any harm in the nursery. Prince Llewelyn picked up his son and held him close, burying his tearful face in the bundle of baby. Then he handed him to one of his men, and bent to stroke the dead dog's head.

"Ah, Gelert," he whispered. "How I have wronged you." He carried the dog tenderly outside, and with his own hands and a heavy heart, buried him under a cairn of stones.

Beddgelert means "grave of Gelert". The village of Beddgelert is on the junction of the A4805 and the A498 at the foot of Mount Snowdon. Gelert's grave is by the riverside and is well signposted along a public footpath. There is a stone to mark the place where the dog was buried.

WALES

ST WINEFRIDE'S WELL: CLWYD

7TH CENTURY

At first Winefride was pleased when Caradog brought her flowers and small presents. He was tall and burly, and the other girls seemed to think he was handsome, but Winefride soon began to wish he would just leave her alone. He kept inviting her to go for a ride, or a walk with him, alone, and she was beginning to find it embarrassing trying to find a new excuse every time. Once she said she thought she heard her mother calling. Once she pretended she had forgotten something upstairs in her chamber. Once she told him her uncle was waiting for her to bring him a book.

Caradog kept his temper under control with difficulty, for he was an impatient and bad-tempered man, better with a sword than with his tongue. He found it hard to make pretty speeches, but he had fallen for Winefride, who was pretty and sweet, so he tried hard to remember he was supposed to be on his best behaviour.

But one day he cornered her in the far part of the garden. She looked around nervously for some way out, but his broad shoulders blocked the way. He took her hand and drew her down onto a bench next to him.

"Winefride," he said. "You know I love you."

She looked down at her lap, and tried to pull her hand away. "I must go," she said worriedly.

"No," he shouted. "Stay here and listen to me."

"What do you want from me?" she asked desperately. "You have not spoken to my father about marriage, so —"

"Marriage!" he cried. "I don't want to marry you!"

"Then let me go," she said. "You're frightening me, and I wish to return to the house. My uncle is waiting for me."

"Then let him wait!" And with those words he grabbed hold of her shoulders and tried to kiss her. She was terrified and pushed him away with all her strength. Caught unawares he tumbled backwards off the bench, and she began to run back to the house.

But he was a big strong man, used to fighting, and furious at being made to look ridiculous. He was on his feet in an instant, and after her.

As she ran, she could hear him breathing hard and catching up. "Stop," he shouted. She ran on. She heard the rasp of steel as he drew his sword, and then she knew no more.

X X X

Beuno, Winefride's uncle, was walking in the garden, enjoying the smell of the roses and daisies, when he heard the disturbance. He heard a man's voice cry "Stop" and heard the sound of running feet. Then he heard a small cry and suddenly all the commotion stopped. Beuno came round the corner of the hedge, and stopped in his tracks.

There stood Caradog, breathing heavily, with a bloody sword in his hand. On his face was an expression of horrified amazement, as though he could not believe what he had just done.

And then Beuno saw the most terrible sight. At his feet lay the body of a young girl, caught in flight, her pale blue gown covering her as gently as the fallen petals of Beuno's favourite rose. But, oh horror! Her head…

Beuno stepped back a pace, so shocked was he. He looked at Caradog, who was clearly stunned by his own dreadful deed. Then Beuno pulled himself together. "Come," he said with as much authority as he could muster. He picked up the girl's head, which had rolled beneath a rose bush, and gasped anew as he recognized his favourite niece.

Through gritted teeth he instructed Caradog, now pale with horror, to hold the body firm, and with infinite precision, he took the head and placed it back on the shoulders. Then catching his own tears with a fallen petal, he used the moisture to stick the girl's head back on to her neck. In silence he held out his hand for Caradog's kerchief and bound it around the slender neck.

With infinite caution the men laid the girl on a bench, and Beuno began to pray as he had never prayed before. Caradog stepped back, and was surprised to find his feet wet. Where the girl's head had fallen, a spring of the purest, clearest water had sprung forth.

Beuno prayed for three hours over the unconscious girl, and sustained himself only with an occasional sip of water from the new spring. The whole household had gathered around. At first they had tried to draw Beuno off, telling him it was useless, but gradually they had all fallen silent, some weeping quietly. As evening fell, Winefride's eyelids fluttered. Then she opened her eyes and looked up directly at her uncle.

"What happened?" she asked in a whisper.

No one answered. It was too terrible to recount. Her hand went up to her neck and found the blood-stained cloth. Slowly she sat up, her uncle helping her cautiously.

Caradog shrank back into the bushes, but Beuno caught sight of him. "Your sons and your sons' sons and all their descendants, and your daughters and your daughters' daughters and all their descendants will be cursed by this terrible act of yours. They will bark like dogs, and nothing save a bath in this spring will cure them."

Then he turned back to his patient. As Winefride and her uncle walked slowly and carefully back into the house, Caradog shrank back, and was never seen again. They found his sword several years later at the back of the rose bushes.

Winefride recovered fully except for a thin line around her neck, and a tendency to sore throats. She became a nun and then abbess of Gwytherin in Clwyd. Both Beuno and Winefride were later sanctified and she is often shown in pictures carrying her head and a palm branch. There is no conclusive evidence of Winefride's existence.

St Winefride's Well, at Holywell, Clwyd, beside the B5121, is situated over the spring where her head fell. It is said to have healing properties, especially for those suffering from nervous disorders. And of course for those who can only bark like dogs.

WALES

THE HYSSINGTON BULL: HYSSINGTON, POWYS

"Plough that field, and have it ready by tomorrow morning."

"But, sir," said the farmer. "It's too large, it is impossible to get it ready in time."

"Then you will be thrown out of your cottage. It's your choice." And with that the squire, a bull-necked, barrel-chested man with thick powerful thighs and a firm large stomach, strode away from the three farmers.

As he passed one of Emily Manson's children in the street, the squire shouted to her, "Tell your mother to come up and help in the kitchen tonight. We have guests."

"My mother's not well today," said the child timidly.

"Well, if she wants to work at my house ever again, she'd better be there," he retorted unsympathetically and walked on.

That evening, Emily toiled in his kitchen, though she had a high fever and the floors seemed to swim before her eyes. Over in the Lower Field, her three neighbours spent all night ploughing, their aching muscles and weary horses protesting at the unreasonableness of the request. But they all depended on the favour of the squire. If he felt like it, he could make them homeless with a stroke of his pen.

The next day, the squire came down to the field to check if the work had been done. "I want it planted up by tomorrow," he told his agent, who had accompanied him. The agent, Josiah Freeman, was a timid man worn down by years of bullying from his master, and he merely nodded. He would pass on the message, with his own apologies. One day, he thought, someone would turn round and attack his master. He hoped he would be there to see it, and he also hoped that whoever it was would not attack him instead.

As he walked up the village High Street on his way to deliver his message, he passed the house of Emily Manson. Her husband had died two years earlier, worn out by the squire's constant demands, and she now struggled to feed her four children, working at the squire's house whenever she could and doing needlework and odd jobs for everyone in the village to make ends meet. The three younger children were sitting sadly on the doorstep.

"What's the matter?" he asked. Usually they were happy, bubbly children, playing ball and getting in everyone's way.

"Our mother is very ill," answered one little girl. "She had to work up at the house till late last night and she wasn't well anyway." Her eyes filled with tears. Josiah did not know where to look. To his relief, looking up, he saw the local priest heading towards the house.

"Here's Father Jones," he said brightly. "He'll know what to do."

Father Jones was looking grave. He was a new parson in the village, but even after only two months in the job he was beginning to understand the difficulty. He owed his position to the squire, but it was the squire who was causing most of the hardship in the village. Soon he would have to confront his boss, and he feared the consequences. Josiah greeted him and then gratefully made his escape.

As he knocked at the door of Gareth Davies's house Josiah's heart sank. He hated doing his master's dirty work. And he knew it was impossible to plant up the Lower Field by tomorrow, even if the men had not spent all night up ploughing it for the master, and even if they did agree to neglect their own fields once more.

Mrs Davies answered his knock. "He's out in the fields, where he should be. And he's only had forty minutes' sleep last night, so I'd mind what I said to him if I were you," she warned.

Josiah went out to the small field where Gareth was catching up on his planting. He gave his message, keeping a wary eye on the powerful farmer. Gareth had straightened up at his approach. "Rot him," was all he said, leaning wearily on his hoe. "Tell him it's not possible. We'll do it next week. If I don't do this field today my children are like to starve."

Josiah nodded, but felt obliged to point out that his master was unlikely to accept this reasonable explanation. Gareth shrugged and turned back to his hoeing. It was obvious he was exhausted and at the end of his tether.

As the agent had expected, the squire did not take the postponement of his work with a good grace. Like a furious bull, he strode up and down his study breathing heavily, striking his thighs with his riding whip.

"Who does he think he is?" he shouted. "I can find hundreds of tenants to replace him, just like that," and he clicked his fat, strong fingers.

"Bring me my horse, I'm going to go and tell him what's what myself. You probably didn't make it clear," he spat at the hapless agent. "Come on, I'll show you how it's done."

The squire, followed by an unhappy Josiah, strode into Gareth Davies's farm after a perfunctory knock. Gareth was sitting in the kitchen with his two friends who were also supposed to be out planting the squire's field. They had just sat down to their first meal in two days and were weary and very hungry. When the squire marched in, Gareth said nothing, just laid down his cutlery very quietly. By the stove his wife, who knew him well, drew a sharp breath. Gareth was an even-tempered man, but if he once lost his temper, the results could be terrible. She knew he was very close to breaking point now.

"How dare you sit here eating? You're supposed to be out planting up my field. Get out there now." The squire swept the man's soup from the table with his riding whip.

Gareth got slowly to his feet. The other men held their breath. The squire suddenly noticed how powerfully built the farmer was. "Get out of my kitchen," said Gareth quietly. "Now."

The squire lifted his whip to slash at the farmer, but all three farmers were suddenly on him. In no time at all he was bundled out of the door, and thrown flying into the dust of the road. As he sat on his backside on the dirt track, unable to believe that someone had finally stood up to him, he heard one of the farmers say, "That's it. He'll never leave us alone now."

"You're right," he said, stumbling to his feet. "You'll be evicted before nightfall. I'll not be treated so. I'll put cows to graze in your garden. I'll make your kitchen a shed for my prize bull. I'll make sure your children are sent to the poorhouse."

"And I wish you were your prize bull," said Gareth. "Then at least we'd know how to treat you. Shut you in a field with a ring through your nose where you could do no harm." Then he slammed the door shut on the furious landowner and returned calmly to his dinner. His wife silently ladled out a fresh bowl of soup.

Outside, Josiah tried to help the squire dust himself down. The man was foaming with passion, beside himself with rage. In fact he could hardly stand up he was so angry. He fell back to his knees and started to paw the ground with rage. Josiah stepped back aghast. His master had always looked and behaved somewhat like a bull, but never had the resemblance been so striking. The squire blew angrily through his nose, snorting in indignation. Still on all fours, he contorted himself terribly, and suddenly from his head sprang two curved horns. Josiah stepped back in horror. As the squire turned round and round in his temper, Josiah saw his coat and breeches rip apart over his shoulders and legs. A long bristly tail, released from the clothing, sprang forth. Kicking aside his shoes, the squire's hooves churned furiously at the dirt path.

"Oh my God," cried Josiah, aghast, and leapt for the relative safety of Gareth's kitchen. As he slammed the door shut behind him, he heard the bull's horns thud viciously home on the solid panels. "It... it's the squire," he gasped, and collapsed onto the flagstones. "What you said... he really has turned into a bull – and he's mad as fire!"

X X X

Luckily the Davies' house was solidly built. The animal raged around outside for a while, banging at different walls and testing the doors at the front and the back. The farmers stood by inside, prepared to defend themselves should he break through, but unwilling to venture forth while the bull was on the rampage so close by.

After a few hours, the bull gave up and they watched from an upstairs window as it set off at a fast trot towards the village, angry steam coming from its nostrils every few paces.

"We must do something," said Gareth. So, armed with pitchforks and scythes, the three farmers and the agent set off on the track of the bull who had been the squire. It was easy to see where he had gone. Everywhere were traces of his passage. Milk churns were overturned. Carts lay on their sides abandoned, horn marks carved into their sides, the horses fled in terror. Flowers were trampled. Frightened faces peeped from upstairs windows.

Outside Emily Manson's house they met the parson. The bull was nowhere in sight, and a few people began to emerge cautiously from their houses when they saw the group of armed men.

"Whose bull is it?" asked the young parson.

"It's the squire," said Josiah Freeman. "Mr Davies sort of cursed him for insisting he plant up the Lower Field. He just got himself in such a temper. And then he turned into that animal."

The other villagers crowded round nervously. "I must say," added the agent generously, "the squire did deserve it." It was the first time he had ever criticized his master openly.

"But what shall we do about him?" asked someone. "We surely can't just slaughter him if he's the squire, as we would a normal mad bull."

Half the villagers looked as though that was exactly what they would like to do, and especially if he were the squire. They looked to the priest for guidance. Curses were the province of the Church, and they waited for his opinion.

Suddenly they heard thundering hoofs, and everyone scattered rapidly. All over the village, doors banged shut and the sound of scraping bolts could be heard. Scores of faces appeared once more at the upper windows watching to see what would happen. Only Father Jones stood his ground, and even he inadvertently stepped back a pace or two.

But now he stood protected only by a large clump of inadequate daffodils and his prayer book. The parson began to read feverishly, trying not to look too closely at the huge animal standing before him, foaming at the mouth, scraping his hoof and lowering his sharp horns menacingly.

"Our Father who art in Heaven," began Father Jones while he desperately thumbed through his book for a suitable prayer. His mind was a blank – he could not remember which prayers one should read to exorcise an evil spirit – so as he reached the end of the Lord's Prayer he just began on page twenty of his book and continued from there.

Six prayers later he was still alive and beginning to feel more confident. He stole a glance at the beast. It had stopped pawing the ground, and steam was no longer coming from its nostrils. In fact it looked altogether less awe-inspiring. He continued to read.

Five minutes later he again ventured a quick glance up from his book. Surely the beast, calm now, was actually smaller? And indeed so it appeared. The priest read and read, and by the time he had reached the hundredth page of his book, the bull was only the size of a large dog. Tentatively the priest put out his hand, took hold of the ring on the small bull's nose and led him down the road and into his church. Behind him he could see the whole population of Hyssington following him in awe and admiration.

By the time he reached the church Father Jones thought the bull had perhaps grown a little again, so he quickly started to read again. Soon the beast was no higher than his knee and shrinking with every prayer. By this time night was falling and although they had lit a candle and he had continued to read, the priest's voice was giving out. He was very tired. Besides the animal was quite tiny now, more like a large rat. He closed the church door, wished the assembled parishioners good night, and everyone went home to bed, satisfied with the day's events. Even Emily Manson managed a watery laugh when her eldest daughter recounted the tale of the tiny bull that had once been the nasty squire.

But as dawn broke the next morning the parson heard a strange sound coming from the direction of the church. Looking out of his window, he saw large cracks appearing in the walls of the building. One of the lower windows had been smashed earlier that week by some boys playing football, and through that broken pane to his horror he could see the huge horns of a giant bull, hurling itself repeatedly at the walls of the church. During the night the beast had grown once more, even bigger than before.

Struggling into his cassock Father Jones grabbed his prayer book and ran to the church. Once more the villagers, alerted by the noise, stood armed with their pitchforks and all manner of pointed farm equipment.

As they threw the church doors open wide Father Jones started to read feverishly once more. The bull charged out into the daylight but stopped as it heard the sound of the prayers. Again it stood calmly and soon they could see it was shrinking once more. Fortified by glasses of ale and elderflower wine the priest read all day. By midday his voice had sunk to a hoarse croak, but he dared not stop.

As dusk fell the bull was once more the size of a mouse. Suddenly Gareth Davies had an idea. He pulled off his boot, a strong farmer's boot, fit for working in muddy fields. He picked up the small animal and pushed it down into the boot, deep down into the toe. The little bull wriggled and snorted in protest, but Gareth folded the top flap down. Father Jones gestured silently to Josiah Freeman and he brought his shovel. The agent levered up the stone slab at the entrance to the church, and together Gareth, Josiah and Father Jones wedged the boot and its dangerous contents into the gap underneath. Then they replaced the doorstep and solemnly stamped it back into place.

The villagers looked at one another. Then Father Jones managed to whisper, "Whatever you do, remember not to lift this step up again, ever."

X X X

You can still see the cracks in the walls of Hyssington church, near Montgomery, off the A488, near the border with Shropshire and Offa's Dyke Path. And no one has ever dared to move the doorstep.

BIBLIOGRAPHY

GENERAL WORKS

Geoffrey Ashe, *Mythology of the British Isles*, Methuen, 1990

Brain Bailey, *Churchyards of England & Wales*, Robert Hale, 1987

Benedictine Monks of St Augustine's Ramsgate, *The Book of Saints*, A&C Black 1989

Henry Bett, *English Myths & Traditions*, Batsford, London 1952

Alan Bignell, *Kent Lore: A Heritage of Fact & Fable*, Robert Hale, London 1983

Katherine M Briggs, *The Folklore of the Cotswolds*, Batsford, 1974

Jeremy Errand, *Secret Passages & Hiding Places*, David & Charles 1974

Joseph Jacobs, *English Fairy Tales*, David Nutt, London 1890

ed. John and Julia Keay, *Collins Encyclopaedia of Scotland*, Harper Collins 1994

The National Trust Guide, compiled & ed. Robin Fedden & Rosemary Jakes, Jonathan Cape, 1973

Ordnance Survey Guide to Castles in Britain, Ordnance Survey 1987

Bob Stewart & John Matthews, *Legendary Britain: An Illustrated Journey*, Blandford Press 1989

John Timpson, *Great English Eccentrics*, BRA 1991

Nigel Tranter, *Scottish Castles: Tales & Traditions*, Macdonald 1982

Craig Weatherhill, *Cornovia: Ancient Sites of Cornwall & Scilly*, Alison Hodge, *Penzance 1985*. BC.

Reader's Digest: *Book of Myths & Legends*.

SPECIALIST ARTICLES
Armada and Drake

Colin Elliott, *Discovering Armada Britain*, David & Charles 1987

George Malcolm Thompson, *Sir Francis Drake*, Secker & Warburg 1972

Alison Plowden, Reader's Digest: *Elizabethan England: Life in an Age of Adventure*

Bath

Bath, Old and New, R.E.M. Peach, Simpkin Marshall 1891

British History of Bath, Anon

Bath, R.A.L. Smith, Batsford 1944

Bath Celebrities with fragments of local history, Jerom Murch,
  Pitman 1893
Thomas à Becket
John Morris, *The Life & Martyrdom of St Thomas Becket*, Burn &
  Oats, 1885
Monsignor Demimuid, *St Thomas à Becket*, Duckworth, 1909
Burton
Byron Farwell, *Burton: A Biography of Sir Richard Francis Burton*,
  Viking 1963
Cerne Abbas
H.S.L. Dewar, *The Giant of Cerne Abbas*, Toucan Press 1968
Morris Marples, *White Horses & other Hill Figures*, Alan Sutton
  Cloucs 1981
David Douglas
Alice M Coats, *The Quest for Plants: A History of the Horticultural
  Explorers*, Studio Vista, London 1969
Athelstand George Harvey, *Douglas of the Fir: A Biography of David
  Douglas, Botanist*, Harvard University Press, 1947
Penelope Hobhouse, *Plants in Garden History*, Pavilion 1992
Gunpowder Plot (Triangular Lodge)
Philip Caraman SJ, *St Nicholas Owen, Making of Hiding Holes*,
  Catholic Truth Society 1980
C Northcote Parkinson, *Gunpowder, Treason & Plot*, Weidenfeld
  & Nicolson 1976
Alison Plowden, *Danger to Elizabeth, The Catholics under Elizabeth I*,
  Macmillan 1973
Jesuits (Sawston Hall)
Alison Plowden, *Danger to Elizabeth, The Catholics under Elizabeth I*,
  Macmillan 1973
Philip Caraman, *Henry Garnet (1555-1606) and the Gunpowder Plot*,
  London 1964
John Gerard, *The condition of Catholics under James I* (London 1871)
Davies Loades, *Mary Tudor: A Life*, Basic Blackwell 1989
Lambton and Laidely Worms
T Arther, *The Wonderful Tradition of the Lambton Worm*,
  Newcastle on Tyne, c1875
S Oliver, *Rambles in Northumberland and the Scottish Border*, 1974
Wilson's Tales of the Borders, vols 1 & 2, 1885

BIBLIOGRAPHY

Pocahontas

David Garnett, *Pocahontas or Nonpareil of Virginia*, Chatto & Windus 1933

Timewatch, BBC TV, 1995

St Andrews

The Romantic Story of the Haunted Tower, St Andrews by the Dean of Guild Linskill: St Andrews' Citizen, 9th, 16th, 23rd May 1925.

St Bees

John M Todd, *St Bega: Cult, Fact & Legend.* Transactions of the Cumberland & Westmoreland Antiquarian & Archaeological Society new series lxxx (1980)

John M Todd, *The St Bees Man.* Talk delivered at various places including St Andrews University Archaeological Society, 3rd May 1995

F C Woodhouse, *The Military Religious Orders of the Middle Ages: The Hospitallers, The Templars, The Teutonic Knights and others,* London SPCK 1879

Tower of London

People's History of the Tower of London (1870)

W G Bell, *Tower of London*

John Bayley, *History & Antiquities of the Tower of London* (2 vols)

James Bartholomew, *Inside the Tower: The alternative guide*

Geoffrey Abbot, *Ghosts of the Tower of London*, David & Charles

And booklets supplied by the sites themselves.

A Shockingly Short History
of Absolutely Everything

by John Farman

Ever wanted to be able to reel off the entire history of the world from one big bang to another? Starting with The Very Beginning, and whipping through the bit Quite Soon After That, The Middle Bit, The Next Bit and The Last Bit?

In this slender volume John Farman does just that, skipping deftly over the boring bits, missing out the dated bits (!) and simply ignoring all the complicated bits.

This book contains 14,555 words, of which:

Napoleon gets 200
Columbus gets 174
Henry VIII gets 87
Newton gets 66
Alexander the Great gets 25
Attila the Hun gets 20
Joan of Arc gets 14
Shakespeare gets, er, 0

"I guess it was just not to be..."
Shakespeare

"Great"
Alexander

"Short"
Napoleon